'You're absolutely gorgeous, Amber... honey blonde hair, cornflower blue eyes, and a perfect figure. What more could a man ask?'

'I... uh... I think you might be assuming just a little too much...'

'Am I? Are you absolutely sure you haven't been feeling the same vibes that I've been getting ever since we met? I would have laid bets that you were every bit as tuned in to me as I was to you.'

How could he have known that? Zach's head lowered and he covered her soft mouth with his own... and by then it was too late to protest because all coherent thought fled from her mind. Her nervous system seemed to go completely haywire from the moment his arms closed around her and their bodies meshed in tingling contact.

Coaxingly, he nudged her lips apart, and the pleasure was so unexpected that she found herself responding dizzily, her mind focussed only on the heated intensity of that kiss.

'If I'd known this was the way it would be,' he murmured, his voice a soft breath whispering against her cheek, 'I'd have made a point of coming back weeks ago.'

Dear Reader,

A summertime romance in the beautiful setting of a de-luxe coastal holiday park – sheer bliss! This one has its own peaceful lake with an island at its centre where the wildfowl nestle and start their own small families. The Cornish scenery tugs at the senses with its rugged cliffs and caves giving way to smugglers' hideaways, while the beaches are blessed with golden sand and intriguing rock pools just waiting to be explored.

An idyllic place to start a romance, perhaps? But that all depends on the emotional baggage people bring with them, and Amber and Zach have more than enough of that. Will they be able to work through their hang-ups and let love in?

I hope you'll enjoy reading their story – the first in a new series of Contemporary Romances written specially for you.

Happy reading,

With love,

Joanna

Dedication

To my family, with love, always

Reviews for Joanna Neil's books:

Harlequin Junkie on **A Doctor to Remember** I really enjoyed this read. Sometimes the tension between Matt and Saffi was simply crackling. It was nice to see her pick up things along the way like she was using her 'muscle memory'. She was a natural doctor, and Matt and Saffi treating children was touching and made my eyes prickle.

Kindle edition of **Her Holiday Miracle** *– verified purchase* Warning! Do not read without handy tissues! This book can be a real tear jerker! However, it does have its humour and lighter moments too! A truly warm and loving tale interwoven with drama and incidents designed to keep you wondering – what – is - coming next! Great writer......great book!

Kindle Edition of **A Cotswold Christmas Bride** *– verified purchase* Beautiful...lovely, family orientated and caring. A great read! Amazing how busy professional people are...but are always willing to help others in need.

Books by Joanna Neil

LAKE VIEW SUMMER

by

Joanna Neil

CHAPTER ONE

'AMBER, SWEETHEART, you worry too much. It might never happen.'

Remembering Matt's easy assurances, Amber curled her pink tipped fingers tightly around the Lotus's steering wheel, and let herself imagine that it was his neck she was squeezing. Matt had a lot to answer for.

On route for the Holiday Park, and the residential block where she was staying, she glowered at the innocent road ahead, and pressed her foot down hard on the accelerator. It wasn't a wise move, she realised as soon as she had done it. On the instant, the unfamiliar car smoothly gathered speed, and for a few alarming moments it seemed as though the hedgerow was flying past. Her mouth went dry, a flush of heat filling her cheeks. She'd forgotten about the engine's powerful response.

Carefully, she eased back again, and wiped a damp palm on the blue denim of her jeans. She was so het up she hardly took in the beauty of the Cornish scenery, the rugged cliffs and the sparkling blue sea in the near distance.

'Borrow my car,' Matt had said, on the rare occasions when she'd needed to go into town. But she'd never taken him up on the offer, and the only times she had driven it at all were to do him a favour and run it into the garage. Her fingers clenched again. Thank heaven that was all she had done. Even then, if she'd known at the time who really owned the car, she'd have had a few things to say!

Breathing deeply, she forced herself to calm down. Letting her irritation get the better of her wasn't going to solve anything, and crashing Zach Berkeley's car had to be the ultimate folly. Wasn't it bad enough that she'd taken over his apartment in his absence, albeit unwittingly?

And that was another thing Matt had to answer for.

'We've finished the renovations on the Lakeside apartment,' he'd said. 'You might as well use that while your plumbing's being put right.'

No mention that it was his brother's property. Right up until this morning, she'd been blissfully unaware that she'd been making free with her boss's place, otherwise she'd have had a fit at the mere suggestion, that was for sure. As it was, just as soon as she'd discovered the truth, she'd had to spend precious hours clearing it up and putting things straight.

It was all very well for Matt to breezily announce this morning that they had plenty of time to get organized - it wasn't as though he was having to exert himself, was it? And she had enough on her plate already, what with the work piling up back at her office in the Admin centre, and the animals for the pets' corner arriving on a daily basis, and the pens still to be sorted.

That last thought had her grimacing all over again. She'd believed Matt when he'd firmly said it would be all right to set aside a wild life area and a pets' corner at the Holiday Park, but now she wasn't so sure. Perhaps Zach Berkeley had ideas of his own about how the land was to be developed? That was the trouble in dealing with Matt. He was so laid back about everything, so supremely confident, you'd think the world lay at your feet, yours for the taking, yet even he'd winced a little, she'd noticed, when he'd heard that his brother was about to descend on them.

Matt kept in touch with his brother all the time, throughout Zach's frequent visits to Europe, or occasional meetings in London, and there were the regular phone calls, but Amber had never met him. It seemed that his fleeting visits to the Park must have always coincided with her short periods of leave. From what she'd heard, round and about, he was a force to be reckoned with, a vigorous, determined business man who had scythed a name for himself in the international leisure industry. She wasn't sure exactly how she felt, knowing that she would be meeting him at last, but one thing was certain - they'd better have everything in order, or they would surely rue the day.

Matt, she recalled, had been deep in slumber when she'd collected the post from the girl in reception this morning. Half an hour after she had returned to the apartment, he'd emerged, still rumpled from sleep, and yawning widely, from the spare bedroom where he'd collapsed after last night's party. It had been a great evening, celebrating the entertainment manager's success in getting a contract with a local television company.

Seeing Matt's groggy state had prompted her to take pity on him and make him some strong coffee.

'I hope you didn't mind my staying over,' he'd said, screwing up his eyes and sipping at the hot liquid in his mug as though it was a life saver. Her mouth had twitched in response. As if he'd been in any state to go anywhere else!

Matt had squinted at the postcard she passed across the table to him and then suddenly he came wide awake.

'Strewth,' he'd groaned. 'That's all we need. Zach, coming here, now.'

'Coming here?' She hadn't expected that. 'I thought he was involved in setting up a new holiday centre in France?'

'He was, but it looks as though the work's finished ahead of schedule, and he's decided to come over to Cornwall and see how things are going on down here.' Matt had frowned as he related the news. 'I wonder if that means he'll want the Spanish negotiations speeding up? When we spoke a couple of weeks ago he mentioned some kind of deal brewing there, and wanted me to set up a meeting with a businessman over there… but I thought we had time to spare on that.' Then he'd turned back to the card in his hand, and something in the slashing black strokes of his brother's handwriting must have cheered him, because he brightened up a fraction. 'It isn't so bad,' he'd said. 'Could be worse. At least we have until this evening to get things cleared up and put back together again. His plane gets in at six, so he won't be here until around seven.'

It was about then that she had the first glimmering of the idea that all was not as orderly in her world as she had so far imagined.

Her blue eyes narrowed as she remembered the way he'd sent a reluctant glance around the kitchen, taking in the litter of empty bottles and assorted glasses, the stale remnants of sandwiches and sausage rolls that spilled over from the lounge next door. When he'd come up against the mountain of crockery, heaped precariously in the sink, he'd shut his eyes quickly, then opened them again, as though he hoped the simple action might have made it all disappear.

'We can soon deal with this,' he'd said airily. It was Matt's way to take a positive view of things. 'A couple of hours, between us, and we'll soon see it off. It only -' He'd broken off suddenly and she'd guessed what was coming as she watched him run long fingers through his unruly black hair. 'What am I saying? I have to check on the hitch with supplies for the catering department this morning. There's no way I can leave it, and… Lord, Amber, the car -' She could still see the way he'd blinked owlishly and knuckled his grey eyes, looking at her with something akin to horror in his expression. 'I'd forgotten about that. What am I going to do? Zach'll go spare if he finds anything's happened to his precious car. He'll be expecting to find it securely locked away in his garage. There'll be hell to pay if he finds out what I did to it.'

'*His* car?' she echoed, her tone ominously quiet, her stare fixed.

Matt winced for the second time that morning. 'I meant to tell you about that. I wasn't doing anything wrong, you know. He said I could use it, occasionally, while he was away. Give the engine a warm up now and again.'

'Occasionally… now and again…' She repeated the words through clenched teeth. 'I don't suppose for one minute he thought you'd extend the invitation to me. What on earth possessed you to deceive me that way? What If I'd been the one to smash the wing?' She shuddered at the thought. 'Heaven knows, you'd better hope the garage have managed to fit a new one.' She was totally out of sympathy with him. 'Shouldn't you give them a call to find out?'

'I'll do that,' he agreed sheepishly. 'Don't be hard on me, Amber, I didn't mean any harm.' His look cajoled, the grey eyes pleading with her tender sensibilities. Then, with a return of his usual jauntiness, he tacked on, 'Will you pick it up for me if they've fixed it?' With supreme confidence, he took her agreement for granted, draining the last of his coffee as he pushed his chair back. Then, absently, almost as an afterthought, he'd said, 'I suppose we'd better do something about moving you into one of the new apartments. Zach will expect to settle in here this evening.'

Matt had been quick enough to dodge the explosion that followed that casually dropped remark, Amber acknowledged tightly as she turned the car off the main road towards the Park. She'd hardly have agreed to hold the party there if she'd known it was Zach's place. As it was, she'd spent the best part of the morning scrubbing a stain out of the carpet and trying to restore order out of devastation.

'But it was the obvious choice,' Matt had protested. 'There's more room here with the extra wing built on, and it meant I could invite more people. Don't worry about it. Zach need never know.'

She hadn't missed the belligerent jut of his chin, though, and his reservations were plain to see when he muttered darkly, 'Anyway, I don't see what cause he has to make an issue out of it. He can hardly throw stones about my getting the most out of life. He's done his share, still does, in fact. It's just that he's more discreet about things these days.'

He'd started towards the bathroom, then stopped and lounged in the doorway, sending her that look of wide-eyed innocence that she was fast becoming familiar with.

'Of course,' he'd murmured, 'if you'd give me just a little encouragement, things would be very different. I'd even think about settling down. You know how I feel about you, and I certainly don't stay in the spare room out of choice.'

She had returned his look with a troubled frown. In the months she'd known him, she'd come to look on him with easy affection, but as far as she was concerned she wasn't ready for anything more. Matt had a wild streak, and though that could be exciting at times, it could also be alarming, and it was one of the things she needed to think about seriously.

'Your timing's way out,' she told him, firmly. 'Just at the moment you're far from being my favourite person. Anyway, I sometimes think that any woman who falls for your chat up lines needs to have her head examined. And there have been a string of those since you left university to come here.'

'Not in these last few months, since I got to know you better,' he countered. 'I'm a reformed character.'

'Are you?' Her tone was sceptical. 'Time will tell. And as for your brother, I expect he knows you inside out and backwards without needing any evidence of what you've been getting up to.'

Matt had grinned. 'You could be right. Perhaps I'd better shape up. Nose down to the grindstone, consideration to the Berkeley name, and all that.'

If she knew anything at all about Matt, his good intentions would last all of five minutes. She only hoped that he'd calm down enough to be safe behind a wheel, because his record so far was worrying. It was the zest for speed that had caused him to crash his own car, and it was the same carefree attitude that had led him to wreck his brother's.

Thank heaven the garage had made a good job of the repairs. She shuddered to think what Zach's reaction might have been if they hadn't managed it, but as things stood, the car had been restored once more to gleaming perfection, and she was thankful she'd had the presence of mind to fill up the petrol tank. Now all that remained was to get the Lotus securely stashed away, and see about removing the last of her belongings from the apartment. At least she had until this evening to clear up the evidence of her occupation.

Driving through the main gates and on past the car park and reception, she reflected that living on site was one of the perks of the job. The staff residential block nestled close by the tourist accommodation down by the lake, and up to now she had revelled in her unrestricted view of the water and woodland beyond. The Lake View Park was set in a lush, green valley, with gentle slopes and a glorious, calm lake surrounded by ancient trees and bushes. She could even stand on the balcony of her two-storey apartment and look out over the sweeping bay in the distance, and watch the gulls search the rockpools for food. Living here also meant there was no hassle with traffic at the beginning and end of each day, and she could usually allow herself an extra half hour each morning to ease herself into things.

Up to now, she'd enjoyed every moment of her ten months at Lake View, and she was thriving on the extra responsibility that she'd had just lately. When Chloe, the office manageress had left to have her baby, it had seemed the natural thing to step into her shoes and fill in, as she was the most qualified, and Matt was more than pleased with the way she was handling things. She only hoped that Zach Berkeley would feel the same way.

She turned the Lotus on to the back road, and saw Jim from Security taking a late lunch break out on the grassy slope by the stone wall, where he could have the best of both summer sun and shade.

He wasn't alone, but she didn't recognize the man who stood beside him, his long body angled against the trunk of a spreading oak tree. Both men straightened as the car approached, and she slowed down, drawing to a halt. As she slid out of the driver's seat, her gaze slanted casually over the stranger. He was a striking figure, there was no doubt about that, and his strong, clean cut features could cause a riot among the women she knew. His hair was dark, black almost, and she saw that his eyes were dark too, a curiously smoky mixture of grey and blue.

His attention was wholly absorbed by the sleek lines of the car, and her soft mouth curved into a wry smile as he came closer. She'd seen that riveted look before, when men zoomed in on the latest motor show sensation.

Turning her glance to the Security man, she said, 'How are things with you, Jim? Did you enjoy your holiday – Corfu, wasn't it?'

'Uh... yes, it was great. Things are just fine, Amber...'

She walked over to him, and they exchanged a few words, long enough for her to realize that he wasn't at all his usual self. His normally cheerful smile was a little strained, and she wondered if it could have anything to do with the stranger's presence. He'd probably hoped to have his lunch in peace, and found himself targeted. It often happened, with tourists who wandered off the beaten track.

Her glance shifted, but the visitor was totally preoccupied, still with that look of keen intent about him. He'd wandered off to look at the car. Somehow, he didn't quite look like a tourist, she decided. It was something about his alert manner, perhaps, or maybe it was the business-like cut of his clothes, the expensively tailored dark trousers that encased strong, muscular legs, and the crisp freshness of the cream linen shirt.

She sent Jim a quizzical look. 'Is this someone I should know?' she asked softly.

Jim nodded. 'He's here to take a look around.'

He would have said more, but the man chose that moment to cut in smoothly, 'This is some car you have here. Does she handle well?'

His voice was deep and sensual, a hypnotic drawl, and she found herself giving him a gentle smile and saying quietly, 'I've only taken it out two or three times.' She didn't bother to mention that each time had only been as far as the garage and back. 'But it feels good,' she added. 'I think I could get used to it.'

The grey-blue gaze flicked over her with laser-like precision. 'I imagine you could.'

Under that cool scrutiny, Amber was suddenly conscious of a flood of warmth invading her cheeks. His sweeping glance missed nothing. From the springy, spiral curls of her sun-kissed honey blonde hair it shifted to the blue short sleeved top, and the blue jeans that clung faithfully to the smooth curve of her hips, then moved down to take in the neat trainers she was wearing. His gaze returned to her face, and lingered for a moment on the soft fullness of her pink mouth.

Her smile wavered. 'Are you here for a special reason, or are you enjoying a day out? This is a little off the beaten track if you're interested in seeing over the Park and all its amenities.'

'I know. I've already taken a brief look around. But I'm here to check out the newer apartments and those that have been recently updated – I have a set of keys with me. Although, it would be better if I had someone with me to answer any questions that come up. I'm wondering if you could perhaps help me out with that?'

'I… I'm not too sure,' she answered. Why would he need to look around? She frowned. Why would he want to look over the apartments? It was true they were expecting an official, a Mr Calder, to come and do his once-yearly inspection of the accommodation to update their star rating, but he wasn't due for a few days yet. Of course, it could be that there had been a change of plan, and Matt had forgotten to tell her about it. It wouldn't be the first time that had happened. 'Actually, I'm a bit pushed for time right now.'

'That's a shame.' Lifting a dark brow, he turned to Jim. 'This road heads in that direction, doesn't it? Perhaps... Amber, isn't it… could drive me over there?' Smiling, he sent her a questioning glance.

'Has the inspection date been brought forward?' she asked, directing her question at Jim. 'We've been renovating some of the apartments, but I'm not sure that all the finishing touches are in place yet...'

'That doesn't matter,' the man pronounced briskly. 'I dare say I can make an informed judgement on things just as I see them.'

She sent a troubled glance in Jim's direction. 'Even so, I'm not sure – '

'It's... uh... all in order,' Jim said, looking vaguely disturbed, and causing Amber to feel even more confused. She looked from one to the other. 'He has security clearance,' Jim went on, 'and I've already given him the keys. He wants to look at the Lakeside apartment first of all – though it's Matt he really wants to see.'

'Don't we all?' she laughed ruefully, thinking of the marathon task she'd tackled on her own that morning, and the lunch she'd missed because of it. 'He had to go into town to meet with our catering supplier,' she explained to the man, 'but he'll probably be back in an hour or so. I'm sorry you've had such a long wait.' So, he was inspecting the staff accommodation as well as the tourist apartments? That posed a problem for her, but she said calmly, 'In the meantime, as you say, I could drop you off so that you could look around, although the Lakeside apartment is occupied at the moment. It might be better if you look at that later on.'

Going back to the car, she gave Jim a farewell wave, then slid into the driver's seat and waited while the inspector seated himself next to her. It seemed, for a second or two, that Jim wanted to say something, and she regarded him absently, but then he apparently changed his mind, and gave a slight shrug. Odd, Amber thought. He usually had a lot to say for himself, but it could just have been that he'd had a particularly difficult morning. Perhaps the inspector had grilled him about the Park.

'It won't take long to get there,' she said to the man as he moved in beside her. 'It isn't far, about a quarter of a mile along this track.'

'I'm right in thinking you had intended to head for the apartments?' he queried, pushing back the seat to accommodate his long legs, and folding his arms across his broad chest. There was a fine matt of dark hair along his tanned forearms, she noticed, and the glint of a gold watch on his wrist. 'I'm not taking you out of your way?'

'No, that's quite all right,' she returned, disturbed to find herself fighting a sudden warm flood of awareness. It had started the moment he closed the door, shutting them in together. It must be his sheer size that had done it. He was around six feet two, she guessed, and what had once seemed like a perfectly roomy interior to the car, had shrunk alarmingly when he had folded his tautly muscled frame into the seat beside her. 'I have some things to sort out,' she added huskily, when the silence seemed to lengthen, 'some bits and pieces to collect from my own place.'

His very nearness was making her nervous, or perhaps it was the way he was looking at her, with a kind of brooding deliberation, that had put her on edge. She fumbled for a while with the clasp of the seat belt until he reached across and briskly slotted it for her. He must think she was inept, Amber reflected uncomfortably, but he made no comment, and it was just as well, because for no accountable reason, the brush of his fingers on her bare arm had made her go hot all over, and she'd have had the devil's own job finding her voice right then to answer him.

She turned the key in the ignition, still conscious of his watchful gaze on her. Perhaps he didn't rate women drivers very highly... the thought unsettled her, but at least it had the effect of making her pull herself together. After all, she owed it to womankind not to make a mess of operating the gears. To her relief, the car slid smoothly into motion and she turned her concentration to the road ahead.

'I assumed from your conversation with Jim that you work here,' he said after a while. 'What role do you have?'

So, the attention he'd been paying to the car hadn't been as total as she'd thought.

'I work in the offices,' she murmured. 'You probably saw the Administration block as you went by reception.' She sent him an oblique glance. 'It's a pity Matt wasn't here to meet you this morning, but I dare say there were compensations if you managed to take a look around the Park. Did you get to see most things? It's a big place to cover in just a few hours.'

'I managed well enough. The new water-shoot looked interesting - and the boating lake has some unusual features... though it seemed to me that a few of the boats could do with a lick of paint.'

She was surprised by his observation. There were one or two that needed slight attention, but few people would have noticed. Clearly, he didn't miss much. 'They're due for a general overhaul,' she agreed, mindful that it was one of the things on Matt's list. A list that was getting longer each day, since Matt found other things to occupy his time.

Slowing down as she approached the first accommodation block, she said, 'This is the beginning of the staff residential complex. Where did you want me to drop you off?'

'Keep going, please, until we get to the Lakeside apartment. As Jim said, I'll like to make a start round about there.'

Frowning, she did as he suggested, pulling up a few moments later outside the prestigious Lakeside apartment. It was set against a backdrop of wooded hillside, and from a vantage point on the front terrace she often caught a glimpse in the distance of the sun sparkling on a vivid blue sea.

'Here we are,' she said. 'It's actually the apartment where I've been staying.'

He scanned the neat, two-storey building, his eyes flickering briefly over the carefully tended lawn and shrubbery, before he climbed out on to the tarmac and walked around to her side.

'*This* is your place?' he queried, his mouth oddly slanted as he bent towards her to pull open the driver's door.

She had no trouble understanding why he found it difficult to believe. He must be wondering what such a lowly worker as herself was doing, living in such luxury.

She nodded briefly, unwilling to go into detail, all too conscious of his strong, male presence and the subtle, evocative fragrance of a musky after-shave that drifted on the air between them.

Sliding out of the driver's seat, she straightened and decided it was time to assert herself, even if it was a daunting prospect.

'Like I said, I've been staying here, and there are still some of my things about the place, so it really would be best if you were to start your inspection somewhere else. I'm afraid you'll have to limit your viewing to the few apartments that are actually completed. No matter what you said before, I really can't let you make a judgement on any of the others. It wouldn't be fair if we received a lesser grading just because you've chosen to arrive earlier than arranged.'

The grey-blue eyes flickered. 'Since my turning up here appears to have upset your plans so considerably, I think it would be a good idea if you were to give me a guided tour. That way, we can both be sure that everything is under control.'

Amber's finely shaped brows pulled together. If she had to spend time showing him around, as he obviously expected, she'd be hard pushed to finish clearing her things from Zach's place. She glanced at her watch. Arranging for someone to stand in for her could take up even more time.

'Do you have a problem with that?' His deep voice intruded on her thoughts, and she jumped a little.

'I - not exactly. But I do have some rather urgent sorting out to do in my apartment. It might be better if I point you in the right direction and join you later.' She glanced around. 'Number Five was finished last week,' she murmured, waving a hand in the direction of a white painted lodge that merged with woodland in the distance. 'Why don't you start over there?'

'I'd really prefer to start here.' He made no attempt to move, and didn't appear to be in much of a hurry to go anywhere. Instead, he looked around, taking in the discreet layout of tourist and staff residential blocks, so that Amber found herself inwardly chafing at the delay. She had to get on.

'Do you have any particular reason for wanting to do that?'

'I understand it's the best accommodation on site, and everything that follows will be judged in comparison.'

'Even so…'

He studied her thoughtfully. 'Would you like me to call Jim and have him accompany us?'

She frowned. It was a sensible offer, meant to reassure her, but time was running out. Zach Berkeley's plane would be landing at six, and she had to remove all evidence of her occupation of his apartment by then. 'Um, no… that's okay. I have him on speed dial if I need him.' Inserting her key in the lock of the front door she hoped that for once it would operate for her without any hassle. It was a vain hope, and her lips set in frustration. Security locks were all very well, but not if they kept out legitimate callers!

'Here, let me help,' he said, taking her by surprise as he came and stood behind her, so close that his warm breath disturbed the silky curls at her nape. Before she could even begin to react, his large fingers had tangled with hers, moving on the key, and the recalcitrant lock had little choice but to give way. 'There's a knack to these things,' he said. 'Perhaps you haven't been staying here long enough to discover it yet?'

Flustered, she smiled her relief. 'Just a few weeks,' she admitted, 'but it's a new lock that's only just been fitted. It seems to be a little stiff. Thanks for your help – though I'm sure I would have sorted it.'

'You're welcome,' he murmured, his gaze wandering over her upturned face, a glint sparking in his dark eyes. She was all at once breathlessly aware that he had still not released her fingers. 'I'm willing to lend a hand any time,' he added, 'though I should warn you, I might not always do it for free. In fact, I think I could say that you at least owe me a cup of coffee, wouldn't you agree?'

'You could say,' she tossed back, 'that you owe me, for the lift. But I'll let it pass, and we'll call it evens, shall we?' She could hardly invite him into her boss's place. 'I don't mean to appear rude but, as I said, I'm getting pushed for time and I really do have to get on. If you want to go and look at one of the other apartments, I'll catch up with you in around half an hour.' She had far too much on her mind right now to allow herself to be distracted, and she sensed that he could do that without any trouble at all, if she was to give him half a chance. There was something about him that set all her senses alight, and that brief glimmer of heat she'd seen in his eyes had fired her defence system, set all kinds of alarm bells ringing. She wasn't going to let herself be drawn to that flame.

She had learned long ago to be cagey about letting loose her emotions, and that had stood her in good stead when she'd had to fend off the advances of various eager young men. Since she'd not too long ago been in a relationship that had turned sour, she had become cautious about getting involved. Young men who were here today, gone tomorrow, were definitely to be avoided, and there was nothing to say that he wasn't in the same category, was there? With his devastatingly good looks he probably took his pick of girlfriends.

'That's a shame,' he drawled lazily, completely unabashed by her put down. 'But you know,' he murmured, 'I'm used to being given full co-operation, and this is, after all, one of the apartments on my list. It's recently been upgraded, the best on site, and it's possible that it might be used at some time in the future for V.I.P. visitors. Who better to show me around than the woman who's been staying here?'

He was certainly persistent, and it followed that he was used to getting his own way. He had full clearance, Jim had said, and she knew Jim well enough to know he wouldn't let her go off with anyone who was in any way a threat to her safety. At the same time, she couldn't think why he bothered her so much, but her hand was still trapped beneath his, and her blood was heating at an alarming rate, just as though he'd lit a fuse. Restlessly, she jerked her fingers away.

'I haven't heard anything about that,' she muttered. 'As far as I know, this place has never been earmarked for anything other than staff accommodation.'

'Didn't you know that Berkeley had it in mind to make changes on this site? Of course, it isn't likely to happen for quite some time yet, so I shouldn't think there's any cause for people to get agitated. He's hardly going to throw anyone out on their ear... unless, of course, they give him good reason to do so.'

'You sound very sure of your facts,' she muttered, a tremor of misgiving shivering through her veins at his casually dropped afterthought. 'Do you know him so well?'

'Pretty well.'

Amber blinked as she absorbed that piece of information, but before she had time to say anything, his hands had closed on her shoulders, and he moved her easily to one side so that he could go past her into the hall. Her nerves jumped in chaotic disorder, her heart beat quickening as she stood for a moment, her troubled gaze following him.

She frowned. Things were not going at all well for her today. The thought of meeting Zach Berkeley might be causing her a qualm or two, but she still had to contend with this man, and right now he seemed to her that he could well turn out to be the more dangerous proposition.

There was something about him that made her hot and bothered, that tugged darkly at her senses at a subconscious, primeval level, and she wondered what she ought to do, now that he had overridden her cautious objections. Jim had given him the keys and free run of the place, but all her instincts were telling her that she should be cautious in her dealings with him. Yet now he was in the apartment, moving around freely. She would just have to be on her guard. She had no choice but to go after him.

CHAPTER TWO

'**THE APARTMENT** isn't at its best just now -' she began, but it was clear he was still not giving her his full attention. He was already moving confidently about the place, with a complete disregard for anything she had to say.

She winced as she followed him into the kitchen and saw that he had stopped short at the sight of the two black bin bags, full to brimming with evidence of the activities of the night before.

'I see you like partying,' he said. 'That must account for the scrubbed patch on the lounge carpet. A wine spill, I guess.'

Trust him to notice! She'd been right in her earlier summing up, he didn't miss a thing.

She decided to ignore his comment. 'The kitchen has been extended,' she pointed out, attempting to divert his attention from things she'd rather forget, and bring him back to the job in hand. 'We've installed new, top of the range cooking facilities, a dishwasher, a washer/dryer, and there are more than adequate power points.'

'Spoken like a true saleswoman,' he mocked drily. 'Did you want these bags shifting outside? They look as though they might be rather cumbersome for you to manage by yourself. So many bottles.'

'It was a leaving do for a colleague,' she said. 'I can manage, thank you,' but her words weren't heeded as she watched him heft the bags towards the back door. He was like a steamroller, relentlessly pressing on, and she decided enough was enough. 'I think I'll go and see to one or two things while you look around. Give me a shout when you're ready to move on to the next apartment.'

She went hurriedly upstairs to the main bedroom. Her cases were packed and ready, standing by the side of the dresser, but there was still her overnight bag to fill with last minute items. There were a few books to be removed from the bedside table, and one or two plants dotted about the place. She supposed she could leave them. Zach might appreciate a homely touch. She glanced over the neatly made up bed, and grimaced. With a bit of luck, he need never know she'd ever been here. Going over to the French doors that led on to the balcony, she opened them and then paused for a while to gaze out at the craggy bay in the distance. It always calmed her to see the natural beauty of the landscape and watch the sea rolling on to the shore. She would miss living here.

'You're looking very pensive,' the man said, from the doorway, and she jumped because she'd been lost in thought and she hadn't heard him come into the room.

'I was just... musing,' she answered him vaguely, half turning, and not at all sure that she was comfortable with him standing there.

'About leaving?' He'd already taken stock of her cases. 'You didn't mention that you were on the move.'

'No... well, that's why I don't have a lot of time to spare, you see. I only found out this morning that this accommodation was needed for someone else.' She walked back into the room.

A brief smile touched his firm mouth. 'Oh, I do see. Better, perhaps, than you could imagine. You still have a few things scattered about the place, is that it?' He came towards her and for the first time she noticed that he had something in his hand. Something white and silky-looking, and... oh heavens...

'These are yours, I take it?' he murmured, holding out to her a lace edged camisole and a pair of fine nylon stockings, and dropping them on to the bed. 'I found them on a rail in the bathroom.'

Heat scorched her cheeks. 'You really don't need to gather up my belongings...' she said. 'I'm perfectly capable of... in fact I... '

'Think nothing of it,' he blandly interrupted, the glimmer back in his dark eyes. 'It's no trouble to me to help you move out. If you tell me where you're headed, I'll see to the cases for you as well. A simple thank you will suffice if you're not going to offer me coffee.'

All at once it seemed to Amber that he was standing far too close to her, reminding her just how vulnerable she was, alone with him like this. She felt for her mobile phone in her pocket, ready to summon help, and began to ease herself away from him, backing away warily, until her legs made a soft collision with the bed. 'I'm not in the habit,' she said, 'of thanking strangers for handling my lingerie.'

'No?' His lips made a mocking twist. 'But you have no qualms about making use of their cars or their apartments, do you? Or am I supposed to assume that your presence in my bedroom is a mere figment of my imagination?'

'*Your* bedroom?' Amber's blue eyes widened as realization made its shocking impact on her senses, and she gasped, her limbs feeling as though they were about to give way. Just as she might have stumbled, his arm slid obligingly around her waist.

'This is your place?' she muttered thickly. 'So, you're... oh no... I thought... I mean, I can explain...'

'I've no doubt you can,' he murmured, keeping her against the hard warmth of his body. 'I'm sure there must be a perfectly logical explanation as to why you've been sleeping in my bed. But I think it can wait.' His grey-blue eyes glittered as he looked down at the soft outline of her parted lips.

'No, seriously, if I'd known this was your apartment, I would never have stayed here. This is all a misunderstanding.'

'One that I'm all too happy to investigate. I'm intrigued to know more about the beautiful girl who's been living in my apartment while I've been away. In fact, the more I think about it, there's absolutely no need for you to move out. I'd be only too pleased to have you stay and share this place with me.'

'Is that so?' Her chin tilted. 'I'm afraid that's not an option.'

'Are you certain of that? I think you and I might get along very well. From what I've seen so far, the way you were with Jim, you're a friendly, likeable girl, and you have a good, professional attitude to your work. And, despite everything, you appear to have a conscience… after all, you did a good job of cleaning up when you heard you had to move out. But alongside that, there's something that appeals to me, especially… you're absolutely gorgeous… honey blonde hair, cornflower blue eyes, and a perfect figure. What more could a man ask?'

'I… uh… I think you might be assuming just a little too much…'

'Am I? Are you absolutely sure you haven't been feeling the same vibes that I've been getting ever since we met? I would have laid bets that you were every bit as tuned in to me as I was to you.'

How could he have known that? It was true, she had never been so drawn to a man as she was to him. It was as though he had some hidden magnetism that acted as a charm to pull her to him. As if he'd read her thoughts he gently urged her closer and imperceptibly, his head lowered so that his cheek brushed hers. She had time to pull back, but she didn't, staying still, spellbound. After a moment's hesitation he took her silence for acquiescence and covered her soft, expectant mouth with his own. He kissed her with overwhelming thoroughness. And by then it was too late to protest, because all coherent thought had fled from her mind. Her nervous system seemed to go completely haywire, from the moment his arms closed around her, and their bodies meshed in tingling contact. The blood fizzed through her veins, roaring against her ear drums as she absorbed the taste and scent of him, felt the warm pressure of his mouth crushing the softness of her own. Coaxingly, he nudged her lips apart, and the pleasure was so unexpected that she found herself responding dizzily, her mind focussed only on the heated intensity of that kiss. A honeyed languor was sweeping through her limbs, persuading her to yield helplessly to that lingering, sensual caress.

Dazedly, she clung to him, her fingers curling into the fine material of his shirt. How could she have been prepared for the way his touch would affect her, for the spiralling excitement, the swift tide of sensation that swirled through every pore of her being? She felt the heavy thud of his heartbeat beneath her fingers, and knew, to her shame, that he must be well aware of the wild, throbbing tempo of her own.

His mouth shifted, explored the delicate line of her jaw, the silken curve of her throat, and sent a tremor running through the slender length of her body.

'If I'd known this was the way it would be,' he murmured, his voice a soft breath whispering against her cheek, 'I'd have made a point of coming back weeks ago.'

His muttered words brought her back to her senses with an unexpected jolt, widening her blue eyes in shock. What on earth was she thinking? How dare he do that? Pushing at his hard chest, she tried to tug herself free of him, until with seeming reluctance, he finally loosened his hold on her.

She ran a trembling hand through the golden cloud of curls that tumbled over her temples. 'You shouldn't have done that,' she flung at him in agitation, as soon as she had recovered her breath enough to speak. The answering glint of amusement in his dark eyes riled her even more, adding to the flush of heat that was already riding high on her cheekbones.

'I don't recall you telling me to stop.'

'I was confused,' she said. 'What were you thinking? I know I shouldn't have been staying here, but I could have explained - you can't simply go around behaving like that... taking what you want, just as you please.'

'Why not?' Zach's dark brow slanted upwards. 'You did, when you took over my car and my apartment. Besides it seemed to me that it was a far more satisfying way of exploring the situation than listening to a lot of explanations, which I've no doubt will not please me at all.'

'I didn't take anything!'

Her glance skittered around the room in the desperate hope that it was true, and that everything was just as he'd left it. Who could tell how he'd react if he discovered she'd made off with his favourite books, or packed his bath towels along with her own? She was over dramatizing the situation, she knew, but he made her nervous just by looking at her. Being in this room with him made her nervous. She still might call Security - he had no right to manhandle her that way. The fact that she had responded didn't come into it...

The king-sized double bed swam into her vision and she went hot from head to toe. He'd already kissed her. What other plans might he be brewing? Conscious of his watchful gaze, she began to edge towards the door, determined to put a healthy distance between them.

'I didn't take over anything,' she repeated in a strained tone. 'Well, not exactly... not intentionally, anyway. And that's hardly the point,' she went on, gathering steam. 'This is entirely different. How dare you imagine you can simply reach out and make a grab for me, that way? I'm not a... a commodity, to be used as you will.'

'I'm well aware of what you are,' he intoned drily, his gaze skimming her outraged figure. 'You're a beautiful young woman and I admit to having let that sway my judgement. If you had been a man, you might have found yourself booted out on to the doorstep in no uncertain terms. I don't, after all, usually return from my travels to find my employees making themselves at home with my property.'

Amber felt the colour drain from her face at the timely reminder. She worked for this man. How could she have forgotten? He was the one who had been paying her salary for the past ten months.

She'd worked so hard over the last few years to get her qualifications in business and facilities management, and when Matt gave her the chance to gain experience at this Park, it had seemed like a dream opportunity, the one she'd been waiting for. She'd even hoped, at the back of her mind, that once she gained promotion her parents would be proud of her... the same way they were of her brother, Nico, showing him the warmth of their love whenever he achieved something. She still yearned for their approval, even though she was twenty-three years old and an adult.

And now... for a few sobering seconds she reflected on what her chances might be of getting another job, without references. The prospects didn't look good.

Even so, her chin lifted on a spurt of defiance. 'If I'd had any notion that this was your property, I wouldn't have used it,' she said stiffly. 'Not for as much as a second, heaven forbid. It's just that the plumbing in my own place is being taken apart, and I had to find somewhere else, that's the only reason I'm here.'

'And this apartment was the natural choice?' He looked unconvinced. 'Odd, isn't it, how I suddenly have the feeling that my brother must be involved in this somewhere?'

He came towards her once again, his stride long and rangy, and she backed out of the door and on to the landing.

'Why didn't you say who you were, from the beginning?' she asked.

'Why should I? I guessed something was wrong when my brother tried to put me off coming back early. He wanted me to stay on in France for a few more days. And then I realized my car was missing from the garage, and Matt couldn't be using it because his was nowhere around. So, I thought it might be a good idea to spend the morning wandering around, gaining an impression of the place as an ordinary tourist might. If everyone had been on their toes, knowing exactly who I was, I wouldn't have been able to get a true picture. As it was, I picked up on several things that should have been attended to, but hadn't, and one or two other interesting matters that need some kind of explanation.' He studied her shrewdly. 'Tell me how you came to be driving my car.'

She swallowed at the deceptively soft voiced command. She could hardly tell him the truth and drop Matt right in the mire. From the looks of things, he was going to have enough of a problem explaining away the jobs he had left undone. 'We... that is, your brother and I... thought you'd be glad of a full petrol tank,' she managed, seizing on the one fact he couldn't dispute. 'Matt was too busy to see to it.'

'That possibly accounts for one journey. Two or three times were the numbers you mentioned, weren't they?'

Ah. 'Yes.' Curse her rambling tongue! 'It... uh... went in for a service,' she told him quickly, thankful that at least, in part, that was true. 'You wouldn't have been too pleased if it hadn't been in good running order, would you?'

'I hadn't noticed anything wrong when I left it.'

'No? Well, that was some time ago, and there was this strange noise coming from under the bonnet - we thought it best to have it checked out.' The only noise had been the clanking of the dented wing, but to tell him that would guarantee sparks. 'It turned out to be nothing at all, of course,' she went on hurriedly as his features seemed to darken. 'Everything is running just fine.' She could feel herself getting hotter as the words tripped from her lips. Since when had she become such an accomplished liar? 'In fact, I've just remembered that I left it outside,' she said, relieved to find an excuse for making a swift getaway. 'I'll go and put it in the garage for you, right now.'

'No, that's okay, you don't need to do that.'

His tone was brisk, and her fingers twisted restlessly against the fabric of her jeans. She could hardly blame him for being annoyed. It occurred to her that he might not have believed a word she'd been saying, but she just thanked her lucky stars he didn't know the half of it.

'Please hand over the keys. I'll do it myself.'

'Are you sure that's what you want?' She hesitated a little as she said it.

'It is.'

She wasn't about to argue with him. He had that certain look about him that told her no one defied Zach Berkeley and came away unscathed. Fishing in the pocket of her jeans, she found the keys and gave them to him.

'Thank you,' he said. 'I suggest you finish what you set out to do, and clear away the rest of your belongings. Pile them up by the cases and I'll see to it that they're removed to your new place.' His brows met in a forbidding frown. 'You have found a new place?'

'Oh, yes. One of the newly completed apartments -' She looked at him in sudden doubt. 'If that's all right, of course? I mean, the workmen are still in mine. They were too busy to get around to it straight away.'

'That's fine. Just go and gather up your underwear and anything else that you've left lying around, will you?'

Heat scorched her cheeks once more. She didn't need to be told twice. He left the room and she quickly started to pack away the rest of her things into her overnight bag.

It was when she was fastening the zip of the bag that she heard the slam of the front door and felt the first faint release of tension in knowing that he'd gone. Those last few minutes had been nerve-racking.

'Amber, sweetheart, are you in there? I see you left the car outside. Looks great, doesn't it?'

Matt. Her relief was short-lived. She groaned, and prayed that he wouldn't say anything to upset her carefully stacked apple cart. She'd just about had enough for one day.

Hurrying downstairs and into the hall, she stopped him in mid-stride, pulling him with her into the lounge. 'It does. I'm not sure your brother appreciated our having it serviced, though.' She kicked him surreptitiously on the shin to make sure she had his complete attention. 'He's around somewhere. Have you seen him? He managed to get back earlier than you expected.'

'Did he? There's a thing.' Lifting her up in a bear hug, he planted a kiss firmly on her mouth. 'You're an angel,' he murmured against her lips, and Amber began to wonder what it was about these Berkeley men that made them home in on her this way. It was very confusing.

Setting her down on her feet once more, he said, 'I can't stop. I'm in the middle of dealing with a problem at the on-site hotel. We seem to have developed an electrical fault somewhere, and it needs to be sorted out fairly quickly. I managed to grab five minutes to come and see how you're getting on, and see if I can find my tee shirt and jeans. I think I must have left them in the utility room this morning.'

'Well, well… You two have been making yourselves at home, haven't you?' Zach remarked from the bottom of the stairs. His dark eyes raked them both, making his own glittering assessment, and Amber was sure he must have seen the kiss. 'So, you've been staying here as well. I wonder how long this set up has been going on? If you add to it the party last night, it seems to me this place has been busier than Piccadilly Circus.'

'Hi, Zach.' Perhaps Matt was used to his brother's caustic manner. At any rate, he didn't seem at all put out by it. 'I gather you've already met Amber.' He slid an arm around her waist, drawing her close. 'She's the girl I was telling you about. Isn't she gorgeous? One look from those big, blue eyes and I'm like melted ice cream.'

'Just take care you don't melt over the carpet,' Zach said drily. 'It's suffered enough.'

'Has it?' Matt was unperturbed. 'It's just that this place has a lot more going for it than mine. I think we'll have to build an extension.'

'Not right now, I hope? I'd far sooner you cleared up the hotel problem first.'

'I will,' Matt answered cheerfully, then added on a more thoughtful note, 'What are you doing here so early? We weren't expecting you for a few hours yet.'

'I'd managed to work that one out for myself,' Zach said drily. 'You obviously haven't checked your email. I sent you a message to say I was catching an earlier flight.' His mouth made a crooked line. 'My coming here ahead of time well and truly threw the cat among the pigeons, didn't it? Given just a few hours longer and there might have been no trace at all of your shenanigans. I think you might at least keep your amorous liaisons confined to your own territory... and restrain yourself from handing out my car keys to any attractive young secretary who happens to take your fancy.'

Amber's harsh intake of breath was clearly audible in the silence that followed that matter of fact delivery. She made to move forward, a few choice comments at the tip of her tongue, when she felt Matt's warning hand at her waist, holding her back.

She glared at Zach, but Matt said calmly, 'I hope you haven't been hard on Amber over this business of the apartment. It wasn't her fault - she didn't know it was yours until this morning. Any hassle is entirely down to me. And as to the car, she was just doing me a favour.'

Zach gave his brother a lancing stare, then turned his diamond bright gaze on Amber's slender form. 'I can well imagine.'

'Now look -' Amber began, her temper rising, 'you can both stop talking about me as though I wasn't here. I've already explained why I was using this place, and as to my relationship with Matt –'

'I can see for myself what your relationship is with Matt,' Zach cut in. 'A man would have to be blind not to see how the land lies on that score. But I should tell you, Amber, I know my brother of old, and I recognize his tactics. You aren't the first woman he's tried to impress, not by a long chalk, and if you've fallen for it, you had better be warned - be on guard for when the gloss wears off, because he's shown few signs of any staying power so far.'

Amber ground her teeth at his brusque summing up of the situation, and turned to Matt, startled to see a slightly rueful expression on his face. For a moment, it threw her completely. Surely there was no truth in what Zach was saying? Matt hadn't set out to try to impress her, had he? He must know that she wouldn't be swayed by a show of wealth and possessions. And why didn't he argue with his brother, put the record straight? Heavens, the man had enough arrogance, he deserved to be batted down.

'How can you stand there and let him say these things?' she hissed.

Matt gave an offhand shrug, pulling her closer to his side. 'He's obviously had a bad day,' he murmured, looking down at her flushed face. 'Take no notice of his irritability - he's always the same when he's been traveling for any length of time. And he's wrong about my staying power, you know. It's getting stronger all the time, especially where you're concerned.'

'I don't care whether he's been in orbit around Mars for the last decade,' she pronounced fiercely, 'and your staying power isn't the issue here. Put him straight about things, Matt...' Then in an undertone she hissed, 'and let go of me.'

'Yes, that remark about the secretary was out of order, Zach,' Matt said with a frown, making no effort at all to release her. 'Amber's very good at her job. In fact, she practically runs the Admin centre single handed and we'd have been lost without her after Chloe left to have the baby. Even your area manager agrees with me on that.'

'I'm aware of Amber's role in the office. I make it my business to keep up to date with who does what, and that includes checking on the way you've been dealing with your own responsibilities. And I can tell you that from what I've gathered about your performance so far, I'm less than satisfied.' Zach's cool glance raked his brother. 'I hope this electrical fault at the hotel is something that you can deal with quickly. Since you neglected to set things in motion for the Spanish deal, I've been obliged to see to the arrangements myself, and Senor Garcia will be arriving within the next couple of hours. I'd prefer it if there were no annoying snags to spoil our meeting.'

'That was quick work,' Matt commented. 'I didn't know you were in a hurry over this, or I'd have seen to it myself, sooner. It's just that one or two things cropped up in the meantime, '

'So I see.' Zach's gaze slid to the arm that still rested lightly around Amber's waist, and he added tautly, 'I do realise, of course, that you might find it difficult to drag yourself away.'

Matt's mouth lifted at one corner. 'You want me to go, and leave her to your tender mercies? I'm not altogether sure I like that idea.'

'But you'll go anyway,' Zach said, his eyes narrowing. 'I've a feeling you've allowed her to divert you from your work long enough.'

Matt laughed. 'Five minutes, that's all. Five times fifty hours would be more the thing, and the truth is, she rates a whole lot more than that.'

'So do our paying customers. And if the boats fall into disrepair, and the hotel facilities go below standard, we shan't have many of them in years to come. Not to mention the poor impression it will make on Senor Garcia if he's unable to take a shower or use his electric razor. This deal is important. If he's impressed he'll give us the go ahead to set up a Holiday Park in Spain. I don't want anything to get in the way of that.'

'Nothing will,' Matt said, releasing Amber at last. 'Why don't you let Amber in on the negotiations? She could be a great help to you, I'm sure.'

'Really?' The slight edge to the word showed the short shrift that Zach gave to that suggestion. 'Isn't it enough that one of us is distracted?'

Amber felt the stab of prickles rising along her spine. He made it sound as though she was some kind of bed hopping vamp. She squared her shoulders.

'You're quite right,' she agreed, coating her words with a thick layer of frost. 'There's quite definitely no point in you involving me in your plans, I'm sure there's nothing at all that I could do for you.'

'Oh, I wouldn't go as far as to say that,' he said under his breath, and there was the faintest tilt to his mouth that made her stare at him with deep suspicion.

'I beg your pardon?' she said, raising her brows. 'Was there something you had in mind?'

At her side, Matt made a muffled, choking sound. 'You know, Zach,' he said, in a tone threaded with amusement, 'I shouldn't be at all surprised if you've finally met your match. Amber's a sweet girl, through and through, but if you try to tangle with her, you might well find yourself on the receiving end of a few nasty scratches. I sometimes wonder if she wasn't weaned on men like you.'

'I thought you had work to do?' Zach's tone was cool, and Matt absorbed the rebuke with a wry twist to his mouth.

'I'm on my way,' he said, 'but I think you should reconsider getting Amber to help you. She's been a godsend to me since I've been down here - I don't know what I'd have done without her. In fact, she's well in line for promotion.'

Zach's expression was brooding as he scanned his brother's face. 'Am I to take it that's what you've promised her?' he queried.

Matt gave a slightly hesitant nod. 'I did. I thought it was about time she was upgraded.'

'To what?'

'Admin Manager was what I had in mind,' Matt admitted. He looked faintly uncomfortable, on the defensive almost, and Amber felt her stomach muscles knot in dismay. She might have known nothing could be as clear cut as Matt had made out, and she couldn't help wishing he'd chosen a better time to air the matter.

Zach was viewing them both with clear cynicism. 'I think I'm beginning to get the picture,' he said, and she knew he was weighing up the fact that Matt had stayed over last night and come up with altogether the wrong conclusion.

'I'm not sure that you are,' she began, and was subjected to a long, hard stare. 'I mean, you might be misjudging the situation,' she added.

'You think so?' He didn't sound in the least bit convinced. 'Tell me, how long have you worked here? A few months? Correct me if I'm wrong.'

'Almost a year,' she said, stiffening as he looked her over, scepticism written into every line of his carved features. 'I've been running the office for some of that time – since Chloe left to have her baby. And I am properly qualified for what I do.'

'I already know about your diplomas, Amber,' he told her. 'I may be out of the country for much of the time, and I might leave some of the day to day decision making to my Park managers but, as I mentioned earlier, I make a point of being well informed about the people I employ.' His glance moved over the bright honey gold of her hair and shifted momentarily to dwell on the fresh, youthful bloom of her cheek. 'It occurs to me,' he went on firmly, 'that you might be a little young to have such a weight of responsibility placed on your shoulders for any length of time. What are you, twenty-two, twenty-three? Hardly any more than that, I'd say.'

'I'm twenty-three,' she answered carefully. 'And I've coped perfectly well with the responsibility for the last several months.'

'Hm…' He looked as though he might give her an argument about that. 'I shall be able to judge that for myself over the next few weeks, since I shall be spending a great deal of my time in the Admin block. I should warn you, though, that the final decision about any promotion rests with me, and you'll find that my standards are a lot higher than my brother's.'

His comment scraped a raw edge, and left her feeling thoroughly rattled. Perhaps it was all she could expect on a day that had started off wrong, and that had seemed to degenerate more with every hour that passed. It all seemed so unfair, because she *was* good at her job. If she had got anywhere at all, it was on her own merit, and not through the matter of her relationship with his brother, though she doubted there would be any satisfaction to be gained from pointing that out to him. He was making his own assumptions and she couldn't entirely blame him for that, given the false picture he'd been presented with so far. Her only real recourse, it seemed, was to let her own subsequent actions prove to him that he'd been wrong.

Matt was going to be no help, that was for sure. He was clearly smarting from that last remark. 'Ouch,' he said, giving Zach a rueful glance. 'You don't believe in holding back, do you? Your teeth can really go deep at times.'

'You've a tough enough hide,' Zach said, unrelenting. 'And I thought I heard you say you only had five minutes to spare? It seems to me that you're needed over at the hotel.'

'Okay, I'm on my way.' Matt lifted a hand in mock submission, heading for the door. 'But do try to keep from taking any bites out of Amber while I'm gone, will you? She's a lovely girl, and if you don't appreciate her, I certainly do, so hands off – she's mine. And I should think again about using her for the deal with Garcia - if she'll let you, that is. She's bilingual. Speaks Spanish like a native.' And with that parting shot, he let himself out of the apartment.

CHAPTER THREE

ZACH SENT her a probing stare. 'You certainly have my brother singing your praises,' he remarked coolly. 'How long have you two been so cosy together?'

Her gaze narrowed. She didn't know what had possessed Matt to make that remark about 'hands off – she's mine' but she wasn't going to give Zach Berkeley the satisfaction of an explanation. He needed to be taken down a peg or two. 'Long enough, obviously, for me to have worked my charms on him. Isn't that what you're thinking?'

'Maybe.' He studied her thoughtfully. 'It's been tried before. On both of us, so, for myself, I tend to be wary of getting too deeply involved. I try to steer clear of entanglements. As the older brother, though, I'm more concerned about Matt, and I feel I have a duty to look out for him. It may not seem like it to you, but we're very close. We lost our parents when he was only twelve years old, and so for a long while after that he was vulnerable and didn't know how to cope with what had happened. It threw him off course for a long time… years, in fact… and he tended to be wild and act out, getting into scrapes. It's still a problem in some ways, I think… he tends to make light of everything and can't settle, so I keep an eye on him.'

'I'm sorry.' Her glance strayed over him, taking in his sombre expression. 'It's true Matt has a wayward attitude to life, but it must have been a difficult time for you, too, surely? Matt mentioned that you have no other relatives to help out, so you must have had to handle everything on your own. You were still young yourself, weren't you… around nineteen years old?' He nodded, and she went on, 'You had to deal with the aftermath of your parents' passing, cope with all the grief and at the same time handle the financial side of things – the house, the business. That must have been a huge burden to carry.'

He acknowledged that with a slight inclination of his head. 'I was shell-shocked, in a way, for quite a while, but I managed. I didn't have much choice… there was no one I could turn to, so I suppose I grew up fast after that. But Matt struggled, and even now he doesn't seem to know what he's looking for. It doesn't help that the Berkeley name acts like a magnet sometimes, for certain types of women. They're drawn to the idea of wealth and status, and in the end it's only the prize they angle after that varies – him or me. I do my best to steer him in the right direction if I see that happening. I don't want anyone to take advantage of him.'

His dark glance moved over her and she inwardly reeled a little. 'Was that comment directed at me?' she asked. 'You think I might be one of those women?' Hearing about Matt's past had been a revelation, because he'd hardly ever talked about it, and she felt an instant sympathy for him, but she didn't like Zach's cool assumptions about her one bit, and she meant to tell him so. 'Well, you needn't have any worries on that score. I like your brother very much, and I certainly don't have any ulterior motive in my dealings with him, as you'll no doubt discover, sooner or later. As to the possibility of finding yourself the star attraction, let me put you right on that, the prize is a definite non-starter. I wouldn't touch you with a barge pole.'

'Oh, you should be careful what you say, Amber.' His dark eyes flickered, a gleam of light sparking in their depths as he took in the defiant tilt of her jaw. 'Statements like that could lead you into a lot of trouble. They might even,' he murmured thoughtfully, his gaze wandering over the pink fullness of her mouth, 'be taken as a direct challenge.'

Her breath caught, locked in the vault of her chest, as his softly voiced threat slowly impinged on her senses. A pulse started up in her throat, beating fiercely as the pace of her breathing quickened. He was watching her steadily, and she wondered why she had never recognized it before for what it was, this look of the predator, the tiger getting ready to move in on his prey. A shiver worked its way across her skin, and she struggled to pull herself together. She had to find a way of dealing with this man, and perhaps this was one instance where attack could turn out to be the best method of defence.

'Only someone with a pronounced streak of arrogance would assume that,' she threw back at him. It wouldn't do to let Zach Berkeley know that he had pierced her armour even in the slightest way.

He laughed softly, coming towards her. 'So, you fight back. Are these the claws Matt was telling me about? Ought I to fear for my skin?' His mouth indented, its firm lines expressive, compelling her attention. He came so close to her that she could see the fine pores of his skin, the faint cleft in the hard angle of his jaw as he stood over her. 'It's been a problem for you, having me around today, hasn't it, Amber? Things haven't turned out at all the way you wanted them to, and right now there's nothing you'd like more than to vent your feelings on me.' His smoky glance swept her features, lingering amusement glinting there. 'Go ahead, try it,' he invited silkily, moving in on her. 'Do your worst, while you have the chance.'

His taunt hung on the air between them; he was so close that she could easily have done as he said. She could have reached out and touched him, run the tips of her fingers down his cheek... her mind shied away from where her skittering thoughts might lead her. That was a dangerous path to tread.

He knew very well what he was doing. He teased and provoked, he wanted her to fall into the trap and she knew - she knew - what form that retribution would take. She only had to tilt her head just a little... His mouth hovered, inches from her own, and she could feel the warm vibrancy emanating from his body, recognized the leashed power that held his limbs taut. She remembered the way he'd kissed her earlier, could still feel it as though his lips were fastened on hers, even now, and she closed her eyes briefly as though that would shut out the memory.

She felt his smile in the warm breath that whispered over her cheeks, and she quickly twisted away from him, sucking air into her lungs to steady herself. He was well aware of what she'd been thinking, and that knowledge burned humiliatingly inside her.

'I don't have time to play games with you,' she said, feverishly conscious that she was retreating in more ways than one. 'I have to go.'

'Running away?' he mocked drily. 'Just when we were getting on so well, too.'

'Were we? I think you're trying to provoke me, and I'm not sure that I fully understand why. I'm well aware that you don't approve of my relationship with your brother.'

'Maybe that's because I think you'd be far better off with me.' Ignoring her stifled gasp, he went on, 'But you're quite right, I'm concerned about him. He isn't functioning at his best, and I wonder if you know why that is? I suspect you do.'

'Matt has a lot of things to cope with right now,' she said quickly, leaping to Matt's defence. 'Lake View is no small thing to oversee - perhaps you expect too much of him and at the same time you forget about all he's achieved here so far? It isn't all that long since he finished University.'

'His role's defined clearly enough, and it's something he's been practising for since he was a teenager. Our parents started out with this one Park, and ultimately, he's going to take over here. It's what he said he wanted to do, and every vacation has been taken up with getting a feel for all of our Parks, seeing how they operate, how they can be improved on. And he isn't alone, he has an area manager to call on if he comes across any sticky problems. It seems to me that he has other things than business on his mind, other things to occupy his time.'

'I still think you're expecting too much of him.' She stood her ground defiantly. 'Matt's only twenty-four and he's still searching for what he wants out of life, whereas you've been at this business for a longer time, and you've a lot more experience than he has.' Matt had told her his brother had worked hard over the last few years to develop the family enterprise into something that was nationwide and international. 'You've worked so hard and so long… your goals are clearly set out, and you simply don't understand anyone who doesn't have their ambitions as tightly honed as you. Perhaps success has made you blinkered. You don't appear to have any sympathy for Matt at all.'

'You make me sound like Methuselah,' Zach remarked drily. 'I've always tried to do my best for him. He must have been conscious of the fact that we were alone in the world when our parents died, no grandparents, no aunts and uncles. I tried doubly hard to be everything he needed, but we both had to face up to the enormity of the situation.'

Amber thought about that. She'd been adopted as a toddler, but before that she had a mother, a father, maybe a wider family that she knew nothing about. Unless she followed the trail of her adoption all those years ago, maybe she would never know where she belonged.

He shot her a thoughtful glance and maybe he was reading something in her expression. 'Perhaps you have some idea what it feels like to be isolated?'

She nodded. Even within her adoptive family she sometimes felt as though she was alone in the world.

Zach said quietly, 'When it happened, when our parents died, Matt and I were staying at a friend's house. They were away on a business trip. Ted's father had to break the news to us that they'd both perished in a yachting accident, and it came as a complete shock, as I'm sure you can imagine. I was worried for Matt. At the same time, I realized that there was no one to head up the business unless I took over the reins. I couldn't stand by idly and see everything they had worked for disintegrate. So, I got on with it, built it up to what it is today, a multi-million-pound organisation. And the reason it works, and stays successful is because I make sure that I can trust each of my employees to do the job they're suited for to the best of their abilities. There's no place for any weak links in the chain, and my brother knows that. Setting up this meeting with Rafael Garcia should have been his initiative. He made a mess of it, and I want to know why... what it was that distracted him.'

His dark gaze shimmered over her, leaving her in no doubt about what he thought the distraction was. She drew herself up to her full five feet four, resenting his implication.

'You're laying the blame at my feet?' Her eyes flashed in scorn, jewel bright. 'I could tell you that you were wrong, but it would be a waste of time, wouldn't it? You've already made up your mind.'

'I don't think blame is quite the word I'd have chosen. I can see perfectly well why he's finding it difficult to concentrate on the job in hand. What I do wonder about, is your motivation, what it is that you really feel for my brother.'

'I already told you – I like him, very much. We're friends.'

'A little more than that, I think. You perhaps forget, I saw you kissing him.'

'Looks can be deceptive,' she informed him stiffly. 'The fact of the matter is, he was kissing me.'

Zach's mouth twisted. 'Is that a valid distinction?'

'It ought to be. And while we're on the subject, perhaps I should remind you that you took exactly the same liberty just an hour before. It seems to me that you should be looking to your own ethics, and not spend time questioning mine.'

'My memory is excellent, Amber. Matt told me all about the new girl in his life, some weeks ago. That was part of the reason for my bringing the business in France to a swift conclusion. I wanted to come here and see for myself just how the land lay on that score. And it's precisely the recollection of those few delicious moments, when you responded so delightfully in my arms, that makes me question just how loyal you are to Matt. You jump right in there to his defence, but I suspect your emotions, where he is concerned, have more complex roots than simple friendship. You have a lot to gain from your relationship with Matt, and I only hope he hasn't built up your expectations too far.'

How could he stand there and remind her of her earlier vulnerability and then mercilessly twist the knife? She'd been right to think of him as a predator. He was lethal, a lurking enemy who waited until the right moment, and then moved stealthily in for the kill. No wonder he'd reached the zenith in the business world. He was utterly ruthless.

'You know, Mr Berkeley, I feel sorry for you,' she said with great dignity. 'You probably don't even realize how insulting your remarks are. I expect they come as second nature to you by now.' Her mouth firmed as she gathered confidence, a soft flush of pink cresting her cheeks. 'It must be painful to live in a world where everyone has to be judged by their material instincts, and I do pity you for that. But I can't help thinking that some of the jibes you direct at me are prompted by your own stinging conscience. After all, you forced yourself on me, and now you've discovered that you were making love to your own brother's girl.' Her eyes narrowed on him, darkly, fiercely condemning, before she added in dismissal, 'But that's your problem. If you're feeling guilty, you'll have to deal with it the best way you can. I can't help you there, and I wouldn't even begin to try.'

'I did not force myself on you. You only had to push me away. And as to feeling guilty about what happened -' His mouth made a mocking line. 'Do you seriously imagine I have no control over my own emotions?'

'It's an idea that takes some getting used to, isn't it? But then, I find it difficult to accept the possibility that you might even have any emotions to bring under control in the first place. Haven't you heard what people say about you? They say you're diamond hard and totally uncompromising. It's beginning to strike me as a rather apt description.'

She had wanted the satisfaction of drawing blood, but his low growl of amused acknowledgement threw her completely.

'You believe in pushing your luck, don't you, Amber? But you might have a point, after all. I do have some conscience, despite your doubts, and maybe I ought to show my brother more understanding and encouragement. I'm not sure, though, that my generosity will extend to open-handedly offering him the run of my home and the attentions of a desirable, willing woman. I would have preferred, I must say, that if you were going to dress up in my apartment in white silk and nylon stockings, you were doing it for me, and not for my brother, or anyone else for that matter. And if that shocks you, it's too bad, because that's exactly how I feel, and as you so carefully pointed out, compromise is not a part of my nature.'

She stared at him, her lips parted on a breath of dismay, her blue eyes wide and clear as the summer sky. She tried to find words, but her throat closed in stunned rejection of them.

'I might also add,' he went on, 'that if you're setting out to impress anyone with your talent and ambition, you'd do far better to concentrate all your energies towards pleasing me.'

She found her voice swiftly enough at that. 'Are you suggesting -?'

'I'm suggesting that you should leave Matt to get on with the job in hand. It's time he made up his mind where he's heading and what he wants to do with his life now that he's put his studying behind him. At the moment he doesn't seem to be showing any inclination to do that.'

'I'm not getting in his way.' Just the opposite, surely? For some time now, she'd been trying to tell him about things that needed attention, but Matt was finding it difficult to settle to anything for very long.

'He came here to be with you when he should have been sorting out the problem at the hotel. Doesn't that give you cause to stop and think?'

'He came for his clothes,' she retaliated sharply. 'He was worried about what your reaction might be. Doesn't that give you pause for thought?'

'That was just an excuse. He came to see you.'

He made it sound like an accusation but Amber refused to give in to his subtle intimidation. Lifting her shoulders in a careless shrug, she said, 'Perhaps he was uncomfortable with the fact that I'd had to clear up here while he attended to his work.' She laid subtle emphasis on that last word. 'He must have known how long it would take to see to everything on my own, and as it is, I haven't finished yet, despite missing lunch so that I could get on and move out before you returned. Believe me, the last thing I wanted was to disturb you in any way.'

He laughed, a short, husky sound, and her head came up, a wary tension darkening her eyes.

'I have to tell you,' he said in a tone of thickened amusement, 'that you failed, utterly and completely in that. From now on, every night when I slide between my sheets I shall be reminded of your presence there. That's more than enough to disturb my sleep for weeks to come, wouldn't you agree?'

Her skin burned as his sensual imagery licked like flame through her veins. He was deliberately teasing, pressing for a reaction, and she mustn't let him faze her this way. He seemed to enjoy baiting her, and she couldn't think why that was, but she knew it wouldn't do to let him get the upper hand.

'I wouldn't have thought much disturbed your sleep,' she muttered. 'You're far too self-assured to allow it. And I can't imagine why you persist in taunting me this way. I'd have thought, with such a vast organisation to supervise, you had far more important things on your mind.'

'But none of them anywhere near as interesting as seeing that delicious blush creep over your cheeks. I'm finding it quite fascinating.'

She wished the floor would swallow her up, but when it didn't oblige, she knew she would have to get away before she made a complete idiot of herself. He certainly wasn't going to make things easy for her. He was enjoying himself too much. The man had a devilish sense of humour, he had more nerve than Lucifer himself.

'I'm sorry I can't stay around and provide you with more entertainment,' she muttered fiercely, 'but I have things to do. There are still a few odds and ends I must clear up around here, and then perhaps I shall be able to find time to have the lunch I missed. If you'll excuse me, I need to get my cases.'

'No, please don't.' He barred her path as she made to go, his arm stretched out, his palm resting on the door jamb, so that she stared at him with sudden misgiving.

Her chin edged upwards. 'I don't understand.'

'I'll see to your cases later and drive you over to your new apartment.'

'There's no need, I can take them myself,' she said, conscious that she had no transport and the cases were cumbersome. Even so, she didn't want to be beholden to him for anything.

He shook his head. 'I insist. Besides, since I imagine it was because of my thoughtless brother that you went without lunch, the least I can do is buy you dinner.' A refusal was already framed on her lips when he added, 'I've been on the move since first light – Matt was right about that - and I could do with a substantial meal inside me. A decent cup of coffee wouldn't go amiss, either, in the meantime. Do you think you could rustle some up while I sort through a few papers for this meeting with Garcia? He'll be having dinner with us.'

His glance went beyond her to the bureau which rested against the far wall, and she noticed a key was in the lock of the writing drawer. It hadn't been there earlier. For the first time she wondered whether he had already been back here this morning while she had been out, and had discovered early on that his home had been invaded. Guilt washed through her veins.

'Yes, I suppose I could do that. I mean, I'll see to it.' She paused, before adding in a thickened undertone, 'I'm sorry about the way everything has gone today. It must have been annoying to come back and find that nothing was as you expected.'

The grey-blue eyes slanted back to her, roaming over her softly curving figure with gleaming appreciation.

'You could say,' he murmured smoothly, 'that there were compensations.'

It was altogether too much. The silky comment shredded the remnants of her composure and she swivelled around and made for the kitchen, his smile burning into her back as she went.

Why did she let him get to her this way, she reflected uneasily as she flicked the switch on the coffee maker? It was unsettling. He must be used to dealing with women who were far more sophisticated than she was, women who had no difficulty at all in handling someone so strikingly male. If only she had their confidence.

The trouble was, she had never met anyone quite like him. She had always prided herself on being calm and collected, yet in the space of just a few short hours, she found her emotions were all over the place. None of it made sense to her. Through the years, she had learned to master her emotions, to mask the feelings of rejection and unworthiness that came from her family background, by losing herself in her studies and in her work. Over time, she had managed to build up her confidence, but now Zach Berkeley had come into her life and everything was chaos.

Tipping biscuits haphazardly on to a plate, she reflected that up to now she had always managed to stay in control of situations, yet since he had appeared on the scene nothing had gone right for her.

The fact that he was her boss made matters infinitely worse. What were her chances of promotion now? Conflicting thoughts chased across her mind as she took a carton of cream from the fridge and prised open the top.

'How's the coffee coming along? It smells good.' Zach appeared out of nowhere, to compound all her feelings of uncertainty.

'It'll be ready in a second or two,' she answered. 'Have you finished your paperwork?' She wished he would go back to it, and leave her to get herself back together again.

'Just a few papers that needed sorting. It's done.' He filched a biscuit from the plate, polishing it off in record time, and she watched him, unwillingly absorbing the movement of his strong, bronzed throat as he swallowed.

He began to prowl around the kitchen, setting her nerves on edge even more, as he lifted lids, checked canisters. He grimaced, then came and stood behind her, his body lean and hard, full of a restless vitality. She wished he would move away. She was suddenly aware of him as an intensely sexual being, a superbly male animal, and the knowledge made her light headed, dizzy almost. She didn't want to feel like this.

He leaned closer to slide another biscuit from the plate, and the warmth from him permeated the thin cotton of her shirt in a way that was shockingly, unexpectedly intimate. She turned towards the cups she had set out on a tray and at the same time his arm brushed hers in a small collision, the contact searing her skin, making her senses reel in frantic disorder.

The carton shot out of her hands on the impact and flew through the air, spraying its contents in a wide arc before it fell to the tiled floor.

Her heart beat accelerated wildly. For a second or two she stared down at the mess, then turned to look at him, dismayed to see that he had been caught in the deluge. Cream spread in a thick, white stream over the smooth linen of his shirt and the dark, expensive material of his trousers.

She watched in stunned silence as the liquid began to melt slowly into the fabric. Then, as her wits slowly reassembled, she said, 'I'm sorry, it just shot out of my hands.' Thinking quickly, she pulled a length of kitchen towel from the roll. 'Perhaps I can remove the worst of it. I'm sorry, really I am.'

Zach frowned at the carton on the floor as she began to dab at his shirt, her fingers making a desperate attempt to put things right. She didn't like to think how much he spent on his clothes. Was his suit ruined? Sweeping the paper towel downwards over the lean perfection of his flat stomach, she sent him a distracted look. 'I just can't believe it happened,' she muttered, swatting lightly at the damage.

'I think,' he said, his voice a little rough around the edges, 'that you'd better leave what you're doing. I can manage perfectly well.'

She stared at him blankly, her mind concentrated on her mopping up operation, her fingers continuing with their feather light brush strokes.

'But I feel so bad about this,' she said.

'There's no need for you to feel that way. It was as much my fault as it was yours.'

He was being generous, and that somehow made her feel worse. 'Even so… Really I -' She broke off as his hands moved down to circle her wrists securely.

'It's okay, Amber. And please stop trying to mop up. I do appreciate what you're trying to do, but I'd rather you didn't…'

'Am I doing something wrong? I'd hate to make matters worse -'

'What you're doing is perfectly sound...' He paused momentarily. 'But you're moving into rather dangerous territory, and I think you've made enough of an impact on me for one day, wouldn't you agree?' Absorbing the puzzlement in her expression, he went on gently, 'You're playing with fire, you know, and unless you care to reap the consequences, which I very much doubt, I think you had better stop right there.'

The wayward gleam of his eyes ought to have been warning enough. Looking down to where he held her trapped fingers, a breath away from the zip of his trousers, the full import of what she'd been doing crowded in on her, and her lips parted on a strangled yelp of dismay. Was there to be no end to the embarrassing predicaments she landed herself in with this man? The way things were going, she'd never dare face him again, let alone go on working for him.

She swallowed hard, and made a conscious effort to still the agitated rasp of her breathing. 'I think I'd better leave,' she said, starting to turn away, looking anywhere but at him. 'I can't stay here.' She couldn't bear to see the amusement which must surely be written on every line of his features. He wasn't helping at all, she registered with a quiver of resentment as she contemplated the way he continued to hold her, moulded to his tough, masculine frame, the space between them narrowed so as to be almost non-existent. Surely, he must be able to feel the thunder of her pulse as it raced out of control? How could he avoid it, and what must he be thinking? She'd simply die of humiliation if she didn't get away. She tried to tug herself free, but his hands moved to enclose her arms.

'I can't possibly let you run away,' he chided gently. 'Besides, I thought it was already decided that you'll be having dinner with me.'

'Oh no,' she said quickly, desperate to make her escape. She flicked him a swift glance. 'I'd really rather not.' She realised how ill-mannered that must sound, and tagged on, 'I mean, I must be going, I've been here long enough, and I still have an awful lot to do. I don't -'

'I was inviting you to eat with me, not share my bed,' he pointed out with sardonic brevity, 'Though, of course, if you should change your mind about that, I shan't be putting any obstacles in your way.'

Her lips parted on a stunned gasp, the blood coursing frenetically through her veins at the mere thought of it. The very idea took her breath away.

'Do I take it that's a negative answer?' he queried in a low drawl. At her open-mouthed silence, he went on, 'Then perhaps we might settle instead for dinner along with Senor Garcia. Not quite as interesting, perhaps, but essential, nevertheless. And since I'm bound to change out of these damp things before we go to meet him, I'd be obliged if you would stay around to take any message that might come through.' Freeing her arms at last, he looked down at her pink flushed cheeks. 'You really needn't look quite so worried. As you're so clearly apprehensive around me, I promise I'll do my very best to keep a safe distance, from now on.'

She thought about that and finally gave a slight nod of acknowledgement. 'Okay.' After all, if they were dining with Senor Garcia, it would be a business meeting and nothing that she need worry about. 'I'll see to the coffee.'

'Thanks.'

Forcing herself to be calm, she cleared up the floor, then carefully took another carton of cream from the fridge, and dealt with the coffee without any further mishaps. She pushed a cup across the table to him and then sat down.

'You said you want me to stay around to take any messages... are you expecting a phone call?' she asked in a tone that was remarkably even, given the circumstances.

He lifted the cup to his lips and drank some of the hot liquid with evident satisfaction.

'Rafael will let me know when he is settled at the hotel, and then we shall pick him up and go and eat. I booked a table at the Smugglers' Bay Restaurant, so we can look out over the sea, and relax in a pleasant atmosphere. This is supposed to be an informal meeting, but it will be helpful to me if you can follow what is said, and pick up on any important points, perhaps type up your memories of the meeting tomorrow morning.' He leaned back in his chair, giving her a brief, assessing glance. 'I take it that Matt was right when he said you were bi-lingual? How did that come about?'

'My father – my adoptive father – is Spanish, so I learned the language from infancy. I don't have any Spanish blood in me.' She wasn't sure why she'd made the distinction about being adopted, but lately the whole question of her background had been occupying her mind a lot. Maybe it was because her younger brother was just finishing his first year at University, studying horticulture, and her parents were singing his praises.

'I see.' He frowned. 'Were you adopted as a baby or later? Do you mind me asking?'

She shook her head. 'No, I don't mind. I think I was getting on for two years old when I went to live with my adoptive parents.'

'Do you have any memories of the time before that?'

'Not really. It's all quite vague… except that it seemed to me that my natural mother was very loving… I remember happy times, laughing with her… it's all fragmented, somehow, but I think we went to the beach and paddled in the sea.' Her expression sobered. 'Though, since she gave me away I suppose that can't have been right. Why would she have handed me over to strangers if she cared anything at all for me?' Even now that thought filled her with sadness and desolation, leaving a bleak emptiness in the pit of her stomach.

'I'm sorry, Amber. Have you ever tried to get in touch with her?'

She shook her head. 'No. I'm not sure I'm ready for that. I might be too disillusioned by the outcome.'

It still haunted her, wondering about her origins, about what had happened so long ago, but she was apprehensive about finding out, afraid of what she might learn, terrified of being rejected all over again.

'It must be difficult for you, not knowing what really happened back then. I suppose we all want to know about our roots. Have your adoptive parents never told you anything about her, or about your father?'

'No, they don't talk about the past. They say they don't know anything about my early years, which I don't think can be true. The adoption agency would have given them some details. I've brought up the subject from time to time, but I get the impression they don't want to discuss it. My mother gets anxious. I'm not sure exactly why, but I know they were upset about not being able to have children initially, and talking about my real parents must bring that heartache back to them and make them feel vulnerable in some way.'

He studied her thoughtfully. 'So, you're an only child?'

'No, that's the thing - I have a younger brother… Nico - he's nineteen now. He came along naturally a couple of years after they adopted me, a complete surprise to my parents. They'd been convinced they couldn't have children, so when he arrived on the scene they were overjoyed.' She made a wry face, looking back on her childhood.

'From your expression, it doesn't seem as though you were too thrilled about that. Don't you get on with your brother?'

'Oh, yes, I do. Don't get me wrong. I love him to bits… he's a funny, outgoing, bright young man. It's just that after he came along I gradually realized I was being edged to one side. I don't think my parents were conscious of what they were doing, but I felt as though I was coming second place in their affections after that.' Her expression was wistful for a moment or two. 'It might have been different if they'd had a girl, I suppose, but Nico was everything my father hoped for – a son to carry on the family name.'

'And he would have Spanish blood in him, too. That must have been a constant reminder to you.'

She nodded. 'I suppose it was. There would be times when they would say how much he looked like his father, he had his eyes, how he had Grandad's quirky grin and how he was going to go far in the family business, because he had a flair for horticulture. In Spain my grandparents have an olive grove,' she explained, 'but here in England my parents have a farm where they grow strawberries and apples, so we helped out a lot when we were young. Nico is good at cultivating crops. I'm not so good at growing things. All my attempts to grow bonsai trees and plant a herb garden ended in disaster. I didn't share any of the family genes, obviously.'

Bracing herself against these negative thoughts, she straightened and brought the conversation back to work matters. 'My parents tried to do the right thing by me. They made sure I had a decent education - I studied other languages, before I went to University, so I can get along well enough with French or German as well. I worked really hard at my studies because I wanted them to be proud of me –

but Nico has their blood and he has a natural intelligence. They're so happy whenever he passes his exams or does well at sports.'

'I'm sure you're equally worthy. You shouldn't sell yourself short. I'm already impressed by what I've heard of your language skills, though I doubt that there will be much of an opportunity to put them to the test this evening, since Rafael speaks fairly good English. In any event, I'm hoping your presence will help to make him feel at ease here.'

'I'll do my best.'

'I'm sure you will.' He paused. 'I'm sorry that Matt has put you in an awkward position as far as the office goes… in fact, he's placed us both in a rather difficult situation… He knows that I have the final say on any staff appointments, so he should have run your job offer by me first of all. Still, I dare say over the next few weeks I'll be able to discover for myself exactly what your capabilities are. We'll be working together for much of the time, and that promises to be, at the very least, an interesting experience.'

She sent him a fraught look, not sure how she would feel if she didn't live up to his expectations, and his dark glance skated over her. 'You don't look altogether happy at the prospect, Amber. Why is that? Does the thought of working closely with me make you nervous?'

'Should it?' The idea of working with him made her wary, but she wasn't about to lay her feelings on the line. Besides, she suspected he already knew exactly what effect he had on her nervous system. The real trouble was, he was fiendish enough to take advantage of that knowledge.

The slow, half smile that tugged at his mouth only added to her unease.

'I think,' he murmured, 'that's a question that promises to be well worth exploring. I'm looking forward to getting to know you better.'

CHAPTER FOUR

'I MUST go and shower.' Zach drained the last of his coffee and walked out of the kitchen, leaving Amber to assimilate a quick flood of relief.

It was high time she got a grip on herself, she decided, rinsing out the used cups. For some reason, Zach Berkeley had a wildly unsettling effect on her, and it was getting to be altogether too much to cope with. Even before he had arrived at Lake View, she had been vaguely apprehensive about meeting up with the man. Everyone seemed to hold him in such awe, and now she could well understand their reasoning. Coming face to face with him had been a real shock to her senses, and she couldn't possibly go on this way.

She hadn't had a good start with him but, somehow, she had to shake off what had happened and persuade him that she deserved the promotion that Matt had offered her. She did deserve it. She was good at her job, and everything was running very smoothly as far as her work at the Admin centre was concerned.

After all that had happened today, though, she had a lot of ground to make up, and going to dinner with him could prove to be a real trial, in more ways than one. She looked down at her clothes. She could hardly go dressed like this, could she, in jeans and top?

Her clothes were packed away in the bedroom, but she ought to be able to find something relatively crease proof to put on. Would Zach still be in the room? There was no reason why she shouldn't slip in and get her things if he was in the shower.

He didn't answer her knock at the door, and when she tentatively opened it, the room was empty. She could hear the sound of running water coming from the bathroom next door, and she quickly grabbed one of the cases and made for the spare bedroom.

Rummaging through her things, she picked out a black dress that she knew would shake out easily enough. It was designed on simple, but clever lines, the bodice neatly textured, the skirt draping softly to outline her shape, and she decided that it would do well enough. Throwing it on to the bed, she kicked off her trainers, then wriggled out of her denims and top, and laid them in the case.

Shoes. Looking through the case once more, she frowned. Where were her black shoes? Hadn't she wrapped them in a plastic bag?

'Have you lost something?' Zach's rumbling query jolted her attention towards the inner door where he stood, a look of faintly questioning surprise etched into the shadowed planes of his face. Slowly, he walked into the room, a towel hooked casually around his waist, his hair glistening with tiny iridescent droplets of water, and she stared at him in disbelief. Her first thought was to grab the dress from the bed and hold it in front of her like a shield.

What was he doing in here? She remembered the dressing room that adjoined this one, and groaned inwardly, then viewed the towel with hot dismay, hoping that it wasn't as precariously secured as it looked. Flicking her gaze hastily away, she encountered the tantalizing expanse of his lean, muscled chest with its smattering of silky, dark hair.

'You were in the shower,' she pointed out shakily, a note of strained accusation creeping into her voice.

'So I was. So, it couldn't have been me that you lost. A few clothes, perhaps?' His glance strayed over the smooth gold of her exposed limbs and the wisps of sinful black silk that peeked out from under the skimpy covering of the dress. 'When I said I'd prefer it if you were to undress for me alone, I hadn't expected you to take me up on my suggestion quite this soon.'

She stifled a moan of embarrassment and clutched the dress even closer. Did he imagine she had set this up deliberately, that she'd been waiting for him to come in here? Was he so used to women throwing themselves at him? If the truth were known, he probably was, and he'd long since learned to deal with the situation and steer clear of any commitment. What was it Matt had once said? Any sign of unwanted entanglement and Zach produced a parting gift.

'I had no idea that you were going to come in here,' she told him huskily. 'I thought this was the spare room.'

'It is. I keep some things in here. A useful precaution, I find, especially for days like this, when the airline has managed to send most of my luggage on a journey to heaven knows where.'

'Oh dear.' She let out a subdued breath. She'd always thought the clothes in here belonged to Matt. 'I'm sorry. That's dreadful.' Even as she sympathized, she wondered desperately if he would turn around and go back where he came from. The air was incredibly hot, all at once, or was it that her temperature had risen out of all proportion? 'It's just that I needed to get changed.'

'Of course. Though, I thought you looked just fine as you were I those jeans that seemed as though they were sprayed on.' His crooked smile played havoc with her nerve endings. 'Not that I'm complaining, you understand?'

Her fingers gripped the soft folds of the dress until her knuckles whitened. 'But Senor Garcia -' She passed the tip of her tongue over lips that were feverishly dry, then collected her thoughts and started again. 'I felt I should at least make an effort of some kind. Surely, it's important to make an impression on him?'

'Dressed like that,' he remarked drily, 'I've no doubt you'd succeed, beyond all his wildest dreams.' He went over to the wardrobe and searched the rail until he found what he was looking for. 'I'm sorry for disturbing you,' he murmured, then he turned and went back into the dressing room.

Amber stared after him running her fingers in agitation through her springy blonde curls as she watched the door close behind his tall figure. This couldn't be happening to her. It was a catalogue of disaster from start to finish and if anything else went wrong she could almost see herself climbing into a cupboard and locking the door.

Despite her embarrassment, she was beginning to experience a growing feeling of respect for Zach Berkeley. How did he manage to keep such an even temper in the face of all that he'd had to put up with? If an airline had lost her luggage, she'd have been profoundly irritable, she was sure, yet he had only mentioned it in passing. He hadn't even been angry when his clothes were covered in cream – he'd only commented mildly that he'd have to change.

Perhaps that was how he'd managed to achieve such dazzling heights in the world of business. He put all his energy into dealing with important matters, and ignored any minor hiccups along the way. Sombrely, she reflected on that. Was that how he thought of her - as yet another, rather troublesome, infraction into the orderly passage of his life?

She washed quickly at the small handbasin, and then stepped into her dress with half an eye on the door, though she felt instinctively that he wouldn't come in here again. Applying a light make up to her face, she added a touch of pink to her lips, and picked up the hairbrush to tame the unruly mass of her hair.

The phone rang, out in the hall, but before she could go to answer it, its soft burr was interrupted, and she heard Zach's deep voice. He was talking fluently in Spanish, and she realised now why he had not been in a hurry to take up Matt's suggestion that she help out. He could manage perfectly well on his own. Her mouth made a faint curve. She might have guessed it; he would leave nothing to chance.

When she went in search of him a minute or so later, she found him in the lounge, standing by the window. She paused uncertainly at the door, a little dazed by the striking figure he made. His deep grey coloured suit was beautifully styled, its expensive cut drawing her glance to the magnificent breadth of his shoulders and his powerfully muscled frame. He wore the jacket open, revealing a self-striped cream linen shirt. He looked immaculate, a man whose strength and authority could not be challenged. There was no disguising the inherent vitality locked within that hard, male body, and, recognizing it, her blood tingled.

He turned towards her, his smoke grey eyes slanting over her. 'Come in, there's no need to hover in the doorway.'

'Did I keep you waiting?'

'Not at all. I've only just finished getting ready myself. You look... enchanting.' His smouldering appreciation banished any qualms she might have had over her appearance. 'Rafael is waiting for us,' he said. 'We'll leave now if you're ready.'

She took to Rafael Garcia straight away. His deep brown eyes were bright and alert, hinting at intelligence and a lively sense of humour.

'*Buenas tardes*, Amber,' he greeted her, holding on to her hand for a fraction longer than necessary and drawing a narrowed glance from Zach at her side. She answered him in his own language, to his delight, and they spoke for a few minutes about his journey and his first impressions of the Holiday Park.

A waitress showed them to their table, and Zach seated Amber in a position where she had a clear view of the bay, with its golden sand, steep cliff faces and rocky inlets.

'Have you settled in well at the hotel?' Zach asked Rafael, as the first course was served. He spread pâté on to crisp fingers of toast and asked, 'Is there anything you need?'

'Nothing at all, I am being well taken care of, thank you. Your brother has seen to all that... and apologised profusely for having to leave me to attend to an appointment in town. It is no problem. I am glad of the chance now, to relax, and my suite is very comfortable, the service is excellent. I am looking forward

to exploring the rest of Lake View tomorrow. You will guide me?'

'Of course, as we agreed.' Seeing his visitor glance enquiringly at Amber, Zach added, 'I'm afraid I can't promise you the pleasure of Amber's company. She's likely to be rather busy tomorrow, in the office. Since she's so familiar with your mother tongue, I'd like her to deal with the translation of any relevant papers. There's also the added difficulty that I shall need her to help welcome my personal secretary to the Administration centre. Liza wants to move to the area, so that she can be close to her family, and though she's highly competent, she's bound to be somewhat disorientated at first.'

He switched his attention to Amber, who was busily absorbing this information while she toyed with her wine glass. 'She'll need to familiarize herself with the office routine, and I'm relying on you to help her with that. Do you think you can manage?'

Amber's hopes were beginning to lurch unsteadily. For so long now, since Chloe left, she had been pulling in the work of two people, and she had done it willingly, thriving on the challenge, and knowing that she was making a great success of it. What would happen now? It all depended on what role he had in mind for his secretary. There was room for both of them, but she dearly wanted to go on organizing things, being the one to make decisions. Did this mean that all she had worked for was about to slip out of her grasp? It seemed so unfair after she had come within a breath of achieving her ambition.

She couldn't say any of this to Zach Berkeley, though. He wasn't going to let her tender dreams influence him in any way.

Instead, she said thoughtfully, 'Of course. I can't foresee any problems with the translations, and, naturally, I'll do whatever I can to make Liza feel welcome.'

'Good. I'm glad to hear it.'

They talked for a while about general things, about Rafael's family in Spain, the time Zach had spent in France exploring Paris as well as the coastal resorts. Zach wanted to know about Amber's parents and her brother, about their trips to the olive grove in Spain, and their life here in Cornwall.

As the waiter arrived with steaks and salad, Zach turned to Rafael once more, and began to outline what he had planned for the following day. Amber listened carefully because he was expecting her to pick up on anything that was said this evening, but part of her mind continued to fret.

She had so many ideas that she wanted to put into practice, and now she wondered if any of them would come to fruition. Matt had always listened, and he had given her leeway that went far beyond her role in the office, a freedom that had always given zest to her working day. She wanted to be part of things, part of the overall administration, and now she could see that she might be reduced to being just another cog in the wheel. Zach had been sceptical about her aspirations from the beginning, and she couldn't really blame him for that, but she knew that sooner or later he would be ready to move on, having decreed what was to happen, and she would be left, drifting aimlessly, unless she could convince him of her potential.

He was telling Rafael about his plans for Lake View. 'I've had it in mind to develop a new pool and sun lounge, on the West side,' Zach was saying, and she tensed a little, her eyes widening as she thought of the plot of land that Matt had allowed her to mark out for the new pet's corner and the children's play area nearby, and then there was the zone that was just perfect for a wild life development.

All the preparations were in full swing, the materials and equipment were on order, and what hadn't already been delivered was due to arrive any day now. It added up to a sizeable amount of money, when you considered the cost of shrubs and trees, specially picked to provide a perfect habitat, and that was before you added on the labour costs. It would all be wasted if Zach had another scheme in mind. They'd intended to set someone on to take charge of the animals, but Matt hadn't organized that as yet. As of now it looked as though all those plans might be shelved. Zach would probably object to adding the cost of an extra salary to the outgoings.

She pushed the salad slowly around her plate. A sinking feeling in her abdomen told her that Matt couldn't have discussed this with his brother, and that her ideas and Zach's were bound to clash. Sooner or later, Zach was going to have to be told about what she'd done. Not just yet, though. Now was definitely the wrong time. Besides, after the way things had gone today, she wouldn't be surprised to find herself thrown out on to the street, along with all her worldly goods. It was a situation that called for tact and diplomacy, and a strategic, if only temporary, withdrawal.

'Is something wrong, Amber?' Zach's stark query thrust into her uneasy meditations, and she blinked up at him, dropping her fork with a faint clatter. 'You're not eating,' he said, his dark gaze homing in on the slender fingers that twisted her napkin. 'Is there something wrong with the food?'

'Nothing at all,' she managed. 'My appetite isn't what I thought it was.'

He subjected her to a hard scrutiny. 'Then maybe we should try to tempt you with a sweet dessert. Something light... a fruit tart, perhaps, or trifle?'

Rafael was enthusiastic about the plans for the pool and sun lounge, and wanted to know more.

Zach obliged, while Amber took careful note and tried to push her anxieties firmly to the back of her mind. He might be talking quite amicably to his visitor, with every appearance of total concentration on what he was saying, but she knew him well enough already to know that there was far more going on in his head than anyone could realize from a cursory glance at him. He didn't miss a thing, he was far too astute to miss the faintest nuance, and she found that knowledge deeply unsettling.

'Has it occurred to you,' she asked, 'that the pool and sun lounge might be better positioned on the South side of the Park? It's a sunnier spot and might be more appealing.'

Zach thought about her suggestion for a moment or two, but then said, 'You're right, it possibly would be, but we have the tennis courts and South side café over there. It would cost more to develop that area.'

Amber absorbed the demolition of her carefully made plans, bending her head to hide her disappointment as she tackled her fruit dessert.

They finished with coffee and liqueurs, and then Rafael excused himself. 'It has been a long day, and I should like to get an early night. I shall look forward to meeting you again, Amber. Perhaps you will both be my guests, next time?'

'That would be good,' Zach said. 'I'll take you home, then, if you're ready?'

Rafael went on ahead, saying goodbye to the restaurant staff. Zach walked Amber out to his waiting car, his hand shifting lightly to the small of her back as he guided her to the passenger seat.

Rafael took his leave of them as Zach drew to a halt outside his hotel. 'It was a very pleasant evening. Thank you both,' he said.

He went into the hotel and Zach turned to Amber. 'You did brilliantly tonight. You managed to put Rafael totally at ease by talking to him in Spanish at the start. I'm really glad that you came along – not just for that, but because it was good to spend time with you. I hope you had an enjoyable evening, too?'

'I did, thank you. And it was lovely to look out and see the glorious view of the bay.'

'It's even better close up. We'll have to go there one day, take a picnic along with us.'

She smiled. 'I'd like that. I love exploring caves and rockpools.'

'Then it's a date.' He put the car into gear and eased his foot on the accelerator. 'I'll drive you over to your new apartment.'

'Thank you. But I need to pick up my cases first.'

'That won't be necessary. It's already been dealt with.'

'Dealt with?' She sent him a bewildered glance. 'I don't quite understand.'

'I hope you don't mind,' he said. 'You should find everything already in place, your cases unpacked, the larder stocked, and so on. You must let me know if things haven't been done to your satisfaction.' Her brows pulled together in puzzlement, and he went on, 'I asked the Security officer to organize things while we were at dinner, since I know that you've been too busy to attend to it yourself. It really wouldn't have been fair to expect you to deal with anything more tonight. It's getting quite late, and you have a full day

ahead of you tomorrow.' He set the car in motion.
'I'd like some notes on this evening's meeting, if you
would, tomorrow, plus a few essential papers
translating ready for me to look at in the afternoon.
Rafael is only over here for a few days and I want
everything to hand, to be sorted out as quickly as
possible. He'll be able to fax the information back to
his office staff, and that should help speed up
negotiations.'

He was thorough in everything that he did, she
discovered. The papers were already on her desk
when she arrived at the office half an hour early the
next day. Glancing through them, she roughly
planned her day's work, thankful that she'd stayed up
last night to work on the notes he'd asked for. At
least she only had the translations to concentrate on.

Liza would need her attention for at least the
first part of the morning. She would probably want to
spend some time looking through a few relevant files
so that she could get a rough idea of the sort of thing
the office handled, and it would save time if she
picked out a batch now. Unlocking the cabinet, she
drew out the ones she wanted, and stacked them
neatly on one side of her desk.

Matt had left her a note saying that he would be
out of the office this morning, making sure that the
boats were thoroughly overhauled. Zach's orders. She
gave a rueful little smile. At least, with Matt away,
there would be no interruptions from that quarter.

Zach walked in as she was making a start on the
post, and she looked up from what she was doing,
her pulse giving an odd little leap as he approached.

He wasn't alone, though, and the woman who accompanied him would have drawn all eyes wherever she went. She was sleek and attractive, a leggy brunette. 'Good, you're in early,' Zach greeted Amber, giving her a smile. 'I want you to meet my secretary, Liza Renshaw. I mentioned to you yesterday that she's moving down here, which means unfortunately, that if she takes to this place, I shall be losing a first-class personal assistant.'

Liza tossed her rich chestnut mane in a gesture of teasing familiarity, her green eyes sparkling. 'I just know I'm going to love it here,' she told him, 'and you'll replace me in no time at all in the London office with that efficient young Barratt girl.'

A tall woman, just a few inches shorter than Zach, she exuded confidence, and dressed with a stylish grace to match. Her suit was cream, set off by the emerald print blouse she wore beneath the jacket. She wore discreet gold jewellery, and her lipstick and nail polish toned exactly.

Amber couldn't compete with her self-assured manner, though the olive-green skirt and lightly patterned blouse she had put on that morning made her feel good. She was glad she'd taken the trouble to brush her hair with extra vigour this morning, though her own tumbling curls would never fall into place in such an orderly fashion as this woman's neat bob.

Liza extended a beautifully manicured hand towards her. Amber acknowledged the proffered hand and said lightly, 'I hope we can make you feel at home here. I'll show you where everything's kept and go through the day-to-day business with you, but I expect it will take a little while for you to settle in.

Don't worry about it, and if there's anything you need to know, just ask.'

'I shall.' To Zach, Liza said, 'Your meeting with Senor Garcia is scheduled for nine-thirty.'

'I'm on my way.'

He nodded to Amber and walked briskly out of the room. Turning to Liza, Amber said brightly, 'I'll show you around and introduce you to a few people, if you like. Then we'll take a coffee break before we start on the main business of the day.'

'That sounds like a good idea,' Liza agreed. 'After coffee I think I should familiarize myself with the various files and computer software.'

'I've already put some files out for you. Help yourself. The ochre folders are the ones you need. The others are ones I shall be dealing with this morning. If you're not familiar with any of the software on the computer, I can lend a hand.'

'There's no need for you to do that. I can cope perfectly well on my own, and I understand you have some translations to get on with, so you'll need peace and quiet. Zach told me that they were rather important.'

'That's okay. I've glanced through them and they don't look too involved. Have you worked with him for long?'

'Three years. We've come to know each other very well – as friends – more than friends, should I say? We have a special relationship. Of course, I shall be sorry to relinquish my position as his personal secretary, but he's really been very generous about everything. He knows how much I want to move down here. My parents have both taken early retirement, and have put all their savings into a small hotel, and I want to be on hand for emergencies, and so on. My sister lives locally, but she has a young family to cope with, and isn't always available at short notice.'

Amber absorbed that information. What did she mean by 'special relationship'? Were they lovers? That thought disturbed her. Even in the short time she'd known him, Zach had managed to stir feelings in her that she had never imagined she might experience. 'Are you staying at the hotel, or with your sister?'

'Neither. Zach helped me to find a small cottage to rent. It's quite close to where my sister and her family live, and only half an hour from my parents' place, so I'm feeling quite pleased about the way everything has gone.'

'I imagine you must be.' Zach, it seemed, could be charm itself when it suited him, and nothing was too much trouble when it concerned the welfare of one of his most loyal workers – or his lover. It didn't surprise her. She suspected that he demanded one hundred and ten percent, but the rewards would be equally high. 'Has Zach said what your job title will be now that you're here?'

'He mentioned Admin Manager, but he said his brother had suggested that position for you, and so he would have to work something out.' Liza looked at her directly. 'It seems that we're in competition with one another.'

'Oh dear. That's not a good start, is it?' Was all her hard work over the last few months to come to nothing? Amber's mouth made a straight line. 'Perhaps he'll find a place for both of us.'

'I doubt that. There's only room for one Admin Manager in a place this size. His brother has the other prized slot.' She walked over to the desk that had been set aside for her, and left Amber to mull over what she had said. The idea of being in competition with this woman left a dull taste in her mouth.

After coffee, Amber dealt quickly with the rest of the post, and then concentrated her attention on the notes and papers that Zach had asked for. It wasn't difficult, but she had to work steadily to get everything finished in time, and she wanted to allow herself half an hour at the end to check things through. She was studying the last draft when Matt breezed cheerfully into the office.

'Still working?' he asked, one brow lifting as he took in the tidy pile of folders on her desk. 'I was hoping that you might let me buy you lunch.'

She glanced at her watch, 'Heavens, is it that time already? I've still to finish checking these – the translations your brother wanted. It'll take five minutes or so.'

'That's okay. I'll wait.'

Amber waved a hand towards her colleague. 'Have you met Liza?'

Matt nodded, and smiled across the room. 'We've met. I hope you'll join us, Liza? I know a little place where they do marvellous food.'

'I don't think so,' Liza murmured. 'Thank you all the same, but I prefer to stay here and carry on with what I'm doing. Presumably I can get some sandwiches from the staff restaurant?'

Amber frowned. 'That's not a problem, if you're sure that's what you want to do?'

Liza nodded. 'I rarely stop for lunch, but don't mind me, you go and enjoy your meal.'

'I wouldn't dream of going off on your first day here,' Amber said firmly. 'Let me know what you'd like and I'll go over there and fetch them for both of us.' To Matt she said, 'Sorry, but thanks for the offer. Another time perhaps?'

Sliding the papers neatly into a blue folder a few minutes later, she pushed it to one side of her desk, satisfied that she had done a good job. When Zach came in, he would have no cause to complain, she was certain.

'All done?' Matt queried, and she nodded, patting the folder. 'Good... we might as well walk over there together,' he said, holding the door open for her when she was ready to go. 'You can tell me how things went on, yesterday.'

They walked across the compound and she gave him a brief outline of the meeting with Rafael Garcia.

'Zach seemed to think you might have wanted to have a hand in organizing the deal,' she said, wondering why Matt had missed the opportunity.

He gave a faint grimace. 'Maybe I would have, but something cropped up, and Zach stepped in. He's good at that kind of thing, but to be honest, I'm not sure that I'm ready to give myself heart and soul to the Company. Zach's a workaholic – I think he's been like that ever since he took on the responsibility of keeping the Company going. Deep down, he's afraid of not doing right by our parents' legacy. Dad always had him in mind to take over at some point... I knew that even when I was twelve years old.' He threw her a quick glance as they went up the steps and into the restaurant. 'How did you get on with him yesterday? He didn't make life difficult for you, did he?'

'He was...' she paused, picking up a tray and going over to the buffet counter, 'fairly reasonable, given the circumstances. But I really think I prefer to forget about yesterday. It wasn't one of my best days, you know.'

Matt grinned. 'There were one or two hair raising moments, weren't there? You did okay, Amber. How did you take to my brother? Most women are knocked for six. I guess it's his looks that do it every time, and that aura he carries around with him, as though he has absolute power over everything and everyone. That wouldn't get to you, though, would it? Your feet are firmly set on the ground.' His gaze wandered over her face and trapped a betraying flush, 'Amber?' he said, a note of uncertainty creeping in.

She looked away. Why did he have to persist in these questions? She didn't want to discuss Zach with him, with anyone, for that matter. Every time she thought about the man and her dealings with him, she came out in a heat rash. It was as though she'd fallen under Zach's spell, been seduced by his charisma. Her reactions were confused, to say the least, and she wanted them kept strictly under wraps.

'I'd rather not talk about him,' she said, topping up her tray with pastries and fruit and walking to the till. 'I told you, yesterday's over and done with, and I have other things on my mind right now. A desk full of work, for instance. And I need to talk to you about the pets' corner and the wild life area. I think we might have a few problems.' She waited while her purchases were stowed away neatly in a carrier.

'Later. We could meet this evening for a drink.' Matt frowned as they went through the glass doors to stand outside on the terrace in the sunshine. 'You're not falling for him, are you?'

'Whatever gives you that idea?' she asked, a little more sharply than she intended. Matt had never been renowned for his perception, so why should his comments be so disturbing to her?

'I've seen it happen before,' he said, a grim set to his mouth. 'My brother has that effect on people - on women. Any encounter with him has them stunned, because when he tries he has a kind of hypnotic charm, but I hoped things might be different with you. Don't go losing your heart over him, Amber. You'll only suffer for it in the end. He's not ready to give himself up to one woman. Besides, he concentrates most of his energy on the business. I think he's a driven soul, because of the work our parents put in. He didn't want to see it all go to waste, and he wants to preserve everything they started. He's been successful, too, and that's brought along its own problems. A lot of women are attracted to the idea of money and kudos, and he was caught out by someone like that a couple of years ago. She made him think she was the only one for him, that he meant the world to her, but eventually he found her out in the lie. She wanted the lifestyle, the jet-setting, and when he was busy working she grew bored and looked elsewhere. She'd been so plausible, he was shaken to learn that it had all been a subterfuge. Probably because of that, he's never shown any signs of wanting to settle down, and I don't believe there's a woman born who could make him change his mind, though several have tried.'

She had thought much the same herself. Zach Berkeley was a man who knew what he wanted and went all out to get it, but she doubted he was ever going to want to commit himself to one woman for life. Why should he, when he could take his fill and then move on to newer pastures?

'You Berkeley men seem to think along the same lines,' she remarked quietly. 'He said more or less the same thing about you. That you weren't ready for commitment.'

Unexpectedly, Matt's arm went around her waist, pulling her to him. 'That's all in the past. I think the world of you, Amber, you must know that. I'm crazy about you. If you'd just say the word, we could have such a great time, we could be so good together.'

She said drily, 'In bed, you mean? I know how you think, Matt.' She shook her head. She'd never been part of the permissive crowd, one of those people who believed in taking enjoyment where they found it and not worrying about the consequences. No. To her way of thinking, that was a dangerous code to live by. She wasn't ready to join the fray and deal with the aftermath of broken relationships. Her instincts cautioned her to be selective, to wait until the right man came along so that she could be sure of her feelings. That way there was less risk of being hurt. For her, everything cut deeper... since her brother had been born and her parents lavished such love and attention on him, she had always felt that she was somehow unworthy of real love. She always felt left out. Perhaps it wasn't logical, but that feeling pervaded her thinking. Maybe she was afraid to test the waters in any relationship for fear of being abandoned, let down. After all, her real mother hadn't wanted her, so why would anyone else care for her? Hadn't her ex-boyfriend shown her that no one could be relied on? She'd trusted him and he'd cheated on her.

As to Matt, she couldn't help being cynical where he was concerned. He was full of sincerity and good intentions now, but she suspected that it was the thrill of the chase he liked, and once he had made his conquest, he would be moving on, the same way he said his brother did. They were very much alike. 'I don't think so, Matt. I'm looking for more than a temporary fling.'

'So am I. I mean it when I say we're meant for each other, Amber. I'd give you the world if you wanted it.' He kissed her suddenly, and she stared up at him, bemused, wondering why she felt nothing, no tiny spark of response.

'Don't you think that the main thoroughfare is the wrong place for that kind of carry-on?'

The crisply spoken rebuke had them both spinning around on the instant. Reluctantly, Matt relinquished his hold on her.

'Hi, Zach.' He recovered quickly. 'Just showing my girl how much I care about her. I'm off to get some lunch. Want to join me?'

'I'm afraid not. I have work to do,' Zach said. Turning his dark gaze towards Amber, he asked, 'Did you manage to get those translations finished? I need to look them over before I meet up with Rafael again this afternoon.'

'They're done.' She wasn't going to let his look of censure intimidate her. It wasn't her fault if Matt tried to make a play for her. 'Were you going to the office now? I'm headed that way myself. I can give them to you.'

'You're not having lunch with Matt?'

'Not today.' She held up the paper carrier. 'Sandwiches, for me and Liza. I dare say there'll be enough for you, too, to stave off the pangs until you get around to a proper meal. I bought an extra pack so there would be more choice.'

'That's very thoughtful of you.' Zach smiled. 'I think I'll take you up on that suggestion.'

Matt lightly touched her arm. 'I'll see you tonight, shall I, as we arranged? I'll pick you up, around eight.'

'Okay.'

Liza was flicking through the contents of a bulky file as they entered the office, but she put it down on her table and smiled across at Zach as he walked towards her.

'How did your meeting go?' she asked.

'Very well. So far, Rafael likes what he's seen. He seems fairly keen for us to establish something similar over in Spain, but he wants to know more about the detailed management and the costings. It's a lot to ask, at short notice, but I'd like to get something organized along those lines.'

'That shouldn't be a problem.' Liza reached for a pen and notepad. 'I can prepare a run-down for you, and let you have the typed copy by tomorrow afternoon.'

Zach was impressed. 'So soon? I might have known that I could rely on you, being efficient as usual. If you can manage it, that will be just great. Ask Amber to give you any help that you need.'

His casual relegation shouldn't have hurt, but Amber felt the stab, all the same, as she turned away to set out the food and set up the coffee machine.

Liza said determinedly, 'I shall manage it just fine without disturbing Amber. I know she has lots of work to get through. There seems to be a backlog, and a whole sheaf of stuff came down from Accounts some time ago, while she was out. It's on your desk, Amber.'

Hearing what the other woman had to say, Amber bit down on a rising sense of frustration. Anyone would think she'd been out of the office for hours, instead of just a few minutes. And, of course, it would be no trouble to Liza to gather together all the information she needed, since Amber had meticulously documented it all herself, on file and on memory stick, the product of several weeks' conscientious work. Liza couldn't have failed to notice that when she had gone through the programs this morning.

'Now,' Zach was saying, 'I'd like to take a look at those notes.'

Amber paused in the act of pouring coffee, and replaced the jug on its stand. Resolutely keeping a check on herself, she handed a plate to Liza.

'Help yourself to sandwiches,' she said. Passing another plate to Zach, she added, 'The coffee will be ready in a minute. I'll get the folder for you.'

'Thanks. I'll help myself to cream,' he murmured, and she thought she detected the ghost of a smile tugging at his firm mouth.

Going to her desk, she pushed the hot tide of memories to one side, and leaned over to reach for the folder, only to draw back in puzzled dismay. The tidy, carefully organized files that she had left there were a complete mess.

'Is something wrong?' Liza asked. 'You haven't lost it, have you?'

Amber searched through the mass of folders, but the one she wanted wasn't there. She checked again, slowly, making sure she hadn't missed it, that it hadn't slipped inside another. She swallowed. 'I... it doesn't appear to be here.'

'Oh dear.' Liza looked vaguely distressed. 'That is worrying. Are you sure you haven't pushed it into a drawer somewhere?'

'No. I'm sure I left it here, on the right-hand corner, by the wire tray.' She checked the drawers all the same, but there was no sign of it. 'The folder isn't on your table, is it, Liza? It's a blue one.' She was clutching at straws, because she knew exactly where she had left it, and something had gone tremendously wrong.

'Definitely not. As you can see, my table is clear, except for the file I'm working on.' A tiny frown creased her brow. 'Why don't you check again? There is rather a lot of clutter on your desk.'

Amber felt sick, and Zach said tersely, 'What about the computer copy? All you need do is print out what I need.'

Nodding, Amber checked the computer. She swayed slightly, the blood draining from her face, so that she felt light-headed. 'That's gone, too,' she said in a voice barely above a whisper. 'It's been deleted, along with the back-up.'

He looked at her, his sculpted features dark with incredulity. 'You've mislaid that, as well? Amber, I don't have copies of those papers that I can readily lay my hands on. I need those documents, and I need them this afternoon.' A muscle flicked tightly in the hard line of his jaw. 'Perhaps you'd be as well to do as Liza suggests. Check every cabinet in the office if you have to, and have a word with Accounts on the off chance that they picked it up. My meeting's in…' he checked his watch, '…less than two hours.'

Conscious all the time of his dark gaze, Amber said evenly, 'I left the folder on my desk by the wire tray before I went to get sandwiches. Matt saw it, because he was in the office at the time. There was no clutter. I saved the file on the computer, but it has been deleted. I can't account for how it's gone missing, but the folder and the computer file were here under an hour ago. Something happened while I was out of the office.'

She looked at Liza, who shrugged and lifted her perfectly shaped brows a fraction. 'I really don't know what could have happened,' Liza said. 'I left the office for a few minutes to photocopy some papers in the annexe. Perhaps someone came in here whilst I was out.'

Amber's blue eyes glinted. The woman was lying, that was for sure. Who else would have reason to show her in a bad light? But she could hardly accuse her when Zach had every faith in his secretary. Still, the battle lines were drawn. At least she knew how the land lay. She reached for the phone with a hand that trembled slightly, and dialled Accounts. Breathing deeply to settle the churning in her stomach, she spoke to the girl who had come down to the office, but the slim chance fragmented almost as soon as it had formed. The file had not gone upstairs. They didn't even need to check, because the girl had gone back empty handed.

She put down the receiver and began to tidy the folders on her desk, putting them into scrupulously ordered piles, and moving them to a work top at the side of the room.

'Well?' Zach said.

She shook her head. Pale, but outwardly composed, she said, 'I made photocopies of the papers first thing this morning. Just a precaution, really. I'll do the translations over again. It shouldn't take me too long. I'm familiar with them now. Just over an hour, perhaps a little more.'

His mouth made a taut line. 'That's something, I suppose. Let's hope you can live up to your words. I'll stay here in the office to make sure that nothing goes astray this time.'

Shakily, Amber sat down and unlocked the drawer where she had put the photocopies. Thank heaven she had taken those precious few minutes to do that first thing. It was something she had always done whenever she had been dealing with important documents, though she had never been in the position of losing anything before this.

Switching on the computer, she let her fingers hover over the keyboard for a few seconds, then thrust them quickly into her lap until she had the trembling under control. She had to do this. She had to put things right, but it was so difficult to come to terms with what had happened. She *had* put the folder by the tray.

A plate of food was pushed across the table in front of her. 'I don't think you're in any state to do anything just yet,' Zach remarked crisply. 'Eat first, and drink your coffee.' A mug of the steaming brew followed. 'That's an order. I won't have you fainting for lack of sustenance.'

He stood over her until she made an effort to do as he said. Though even the thought of food was nauseating at first, it was surprising how quickly it helped her to get back to somewhere near normal. Seeing her comply with his request, he gave a nod of satisfaction. 'Are you feeling a bit better?'

She nodded, grateful for his understanding.

'Good.' He walked over to Liza's desk and began to talk to her about his afternoon schedule.

Amber started work on the papers once more, all too aware of Zach across the room, half-sitting, half-leaning on Liza's table, chatting quietly, an easy familiarity between the pair. How close were they? She kept her head down and forced herself to concentrate on what she was doing.

An hour later, she had finished. Relieved, she checked the papers through and then handed them to Zach, who scanned each page with meticulous care.

'Thank you,' he said. 'Tomorrow, I have another meeting at eleven, but before then I want to go through one or two things with you and Matt. Keep the first part of the morning free, if you will. I want to make an early start.'

He went over to Liza and placed a hand lightly on her shoulder. 'Dinner this evening?' he asked, and she nodded, smiling.

'I'd love to. But we don't need to go out. Why don't you come over to my place, and I'll prepare something special?' Beneath his jacket, he flexed shoulder muscles, relaxing, and returned her smile with careless intimacy. 'That's the kind of invitation I can't refuse,' he murmured.

Amber looked away. Why did it bother her so much, knowing that he would be spending the evening with Liza Renshaw? Because it did trouble her. A lot. It was a physical pain that knotted her stomach and constricted her throat, and it left her feeling wretched, knowing that evening always stretched into night, and she wondered where Zach would be spending the night, in whose arms?

CHAPTER FIVE

'MATT, YOU ought to start heading for the office. You'll be late. There's no need for both of us to get into trouble.'

There was an edginess about Amber's voice as she said it, and at the same time she threw a harried look around the copse. She was responsible for the pets' corner that was being set up and things were already going wrong. She had gone to check on the goat's stall first thing this morning, and the goat was nowhere to be seen.

Sunlight dappled the leaves and warmed the gentle grassy slopes, and she put up a hand to shield her eyes while she squinted through the trees. If the sun was strong this early in the day, it promised to be hot later. The holidaymakers would love it, those of them who went out and about to explore the Cornish hills and dales, or spent time on the sandy beach that was just a short walk away.

In the meantime, there was no sign of the goat. She could really do without this problem right now, and if the workmen had fixed the fence to the height she'd requested, the animal would never have escaped to go wandering in the first place. Common sense should have told them the pen wasn't adequate. After all, everyone knew goats could jump, didn't they? With all that had happened yesterday, she hadn't had a moment to check what the workmen had done, and she'd delegated the task, which only served her right. She ought to have known that was a risky thing to do, considering the way things had been going for her just lately.

'I'll manage here,' she said, worrying about Matt, who hadn't made a move to go. 'You don't have to stay.'

She might have been sitting behind her desk now, ready to face whatever the day - whatever Zach had in store for her, but she ought to have known from the outset that there was little chance of that. Everything she planned seemed to go wrong, just lately.

True, she'd made some headway with the work she'd taken home last night. That influx of papers from Accounts had been on her mind, and she'd left Matt after just a couple of drinks, so that she could work on them. Even so, she'd only managed to deal with half of them, and she'd been up since the crack of dawn trying to go through the rest. Then Jim's dropping by to tell her about the goat's breakout had put a stop to that, and it had been a race against time from then on.

She rubbed a hand wearily across her forehead. It seemed that fate was playing impish games with her, and what had once been a reasonably calm and uneventful existence was now spinning riotously out of control.

'Hey, I'm here to help,' Matt said, and she smiled at him.

'Thanks.'

'You're more than welcome. I hate to see you looking so stressed.' He wrapped his arms around her and kissed her briefly. 'Could we meet up tonight, have a drink together, and maybe grab a bite to eat?'

Amber nodded and gave him a hug in return. 'Okay, I'd like that.' Perhaps she ought to consider dating Matt properly. She felt safe with him, well within her comfort zone. She had the feeling he would never let her down where his feelings for her were concerned. He would always be there for her.

'That's great.' He glanced at his watch. 'You're going to be late, too. It's well after nine. We should get a move on.'

'Yes, but I'm already in trouble with Zach on several counts, and one more isn't going to make that much difference.' She winced inwardly at the thought. Going on yesterday's debacle, she was probably doomed whatever she did. She could only cling to the fragile hope that Zach might be late getting to the office, and not know that she wasn't there on time.

'What kind of trouble?'

'Oh, those translations I did for him went missing, and it almost made him late for a meeting. He wasn't very pleased, to say the least. I don't suppose I would have been, either, had the situation been reversed.' She sighed, a little wistfully. 'He has a lot of energy and drive, doesn't he? He likes to get things done, and inefficiency irritates him. I seem to be getting on the wrong side of him all the time.'

'You're never inefficient,' Matt declared summarily dismissing her anxieties, 'and I feel sure Zach would never blame anyone out of hand. You shouldn't worry. He'll have looked at the situation from every angle, and he'll know that what happened wasn't your fault.'

Her face set in a glum expression. 'I wish I could be so sure.' The missing folder had resolutely stayed undercover... probably in Liza's roomy bag. 'Anyway,' she said, trying to shake off the blues, 'you should go. Like I said earlier, he wanted to see us both this morning before his meeting, so he'll probably be waiting for you, and you really ought to hurry along and hear what he has to say. He's given you the opportunity to run this place, and you could make something of it, put your own stamp on it. If you don't make decisions, your brother will make them for you, and it shouldn't be like that. You should make up your mind what it is that you want.'

'I don't know what I want. Except -' he broke off and pointed towards the far side of the copse. 'There's the goat. He's eating the grass by the fence. Bring the rope, Amber, and we'll trap him there and tether him to the post. You cut him off to the left, and I'll go this way.'

He moved off at an angle, and Amber followed cautiously, trying to be silent so that the animal wouldn't hear her approach. She was beginning to wish she'd never thought up the idea of this pets' corner. The way things were heading, it was going to land her in all kinds of trouble.

'Got him.' Matt dived at the startled goat and grabbed him, while Amber looped the rope around his neck and fastened the other end to the fence.

'I'll get the workmen to fix the pen and I'll arrange for him to be installed properly,' she said, as they made their way at last to the office block. 'You go on, while I get things sorted out.'

It took a matter of minutes to organize things, but when she came away from reception, she discovered that Matt was still waiting for her.

'We'll beard the lion in his den together,' he told her, coming into step beside her. 'I'm used to Zach, but he obviously has an odd effect on you.' He slipped an arm around her shoulders. 'You shouldn't let his growling get to you. His teeth are sharp, but he isn't likely to savage an innocent soul like you.'

She wouldn't have liked to take bets on that, and when Matt pushed open the door to the office and she saw that Zach was already there, sifting through the day's post, she felt like turning around and walking right out again. Her head was already muzzy from lack of sleep, and she had the strong feeling that she would need all her wits about her if she was to cope with him today.

He wasn't wearing the jacket to his suit. That was casually draped over the back of a chair, and she guessed he'd probably been in the office for some time. He had his shirt sleeves rolled back, exposing strong brown forearms, and he looked powerfully assured, as usual, his lean height making the room seem somehow diminished in size. He radiated energy, a kind of sexual charge that made him intensely male, and yet there was a remoteness about

100

him that made her wish she could reach out to him and tear down the armour he kept around himself. Because it *was* a defensive shield, she was sure of it.

The thought fled in a wave of heat as his penetrating gaze met her full force. Liza was seated behind a desk, a disdainful little smile playing around her mouth as she watched them enter the room. She must know how annoyed Zach was, because of their lateness; how could she not, when the vibes were slicing the air like balls on a squash court.

She wondered what gave Liza the right to feel smug, then mulled over last night's cosy little set-up, and sent the thought skidding on its way. It still troubled her to think of them together.

She lifted her chin a fraction, her fingers curling into the cloth of her skirt. Whatever was in store, she wasn't going to slump under the onslaught, especially not in front of his conniving secretary.

'Liza,' Zach said, 'I'd like you to go over to the Security office and check on the new arrangements we discussed with Jim yesterday. See if he's set things in motion, please.'

'Right now?' Liza looked a trifle put out. 'I thought –'

'Now, please.' His tone brooked no argument, and Liza placed her notepad carefully on the table.

'Very well. Though, you said you needed to take a look at the ledger I mentioned.'

'I shall. But there's no reason for you to stay. I've no doubt Amber can go through it with me.'

Liza smiled at him, and gracefully got to her feet. 'You're right, of course. She'll probably be able to explain everything.'

Amber frowned. What now? What was Liza cooking up in that scheming brain of hers?

Liza brushed past them as she went through the door, closing it behind her, and Amber took a deep breath, feeling the full force of Zach's scrutiny on her.

'I'm sorry I'm late,' she began.

'We were held up,' Matt said. 'Couldn't be avoided, I'm afraid. A little domestic difficulty, you might say. As it is, we've had a real rush to get here.'

'Have you? Perhaps I should be glad that you found the time to turn up at all for work today.' Zach's stare homed in on Matt's arm, still casually draped around Amber's shoulders. 'How tedious of me to drag you in here. I'd hate to feel that I was interrupting your social life.'

'Sarcasm,' Matt said, leaving her side and going to lean against the filing cabinet, 'is the lowest form of wit. And I'll have you know that you've done nothing but interrupt my social life since you arrived here. Last night was the first chance I've had to get Amber to myself in the last few days.'

'Really?' Zach's cool gaze swung towards Amber. 'I hope you haven't been feeling too deprived?'

His strafing comments were meant to sting, but she braced herself against them.

'I can explain,' she said. 'I did try to get here for nine, but there was a problem, a situation I had to deal with, and when Matt found out about it, he came to help. I'll make up the time, of course.'

'That won't be necessary.' His glance ran over her, broodingly taking in the dark-coloured blouse and slim fitting cream linen skirt she wore, sliding over her smooth, shapely legs and the high heeled shoes she was wearing. The searching, thorough appraisal warmed her skin, left her throat uncomfortably dry. 'Since, from what I gather, you've been running this centre single-handedly for the last few months,' he said, 'you've probably put in more than your fair share of overtime. All of which could have been avoided, of course, if my brother had taken the trouble to arrange for a temp to come in and help out.'

'Amber was doing fine on her own,' Matt intervened. He drew her close, smiling down at her.

'We must assume so,' Zach said, watching the action and frowning. 'Otherwise I imagine we'd have found ourselves in the middle of an almighty shambles, by now. As it is I realize she's organized things so that Liza has Senor Garcia's costings information at her fingertips.'

Amber blinked. So he knew that it was her work that Liza had taken credit for.

Zach returned his attention to Amber once more. 'I understand you keep a detailed ledger of all purchases that have been made over the last three months. Would you mind getting it for me? Liza tells me there are some rather ambiguous items I should take a look at. You could perhaps clarify them for me.'

She swallowed, a throb of unease beginning to pound at her temples. Ambiguous? Had Liza picked up on her equipment order already? Trust her to point it out to him. A wave of weary acceptance washed over her, and she lifted her fingertips to slowly rub at the source of pain. She'd hoped for just a little more time... time to choose a suitable moment to explain about the pets' corner, and she had the feeling that this wasn't quite it.

'You look pale, Amber. Not the result of too many late nights, I hope?' He looked from her to Matt, and back again, his voice showing not one shred of sympathy. 'Do tell me if I'm keeping you both awake.'

He was fiendishly sharp, and it simply wasn't fair. He had the wrong idea about what was going on, and Matt wasn't helping at all. He just stood there with a lop-sided grin on his face as though he found the whole thing amusing. He wanted his brother to think there was more to their relationship than there really was, and it was making her life doubly difficult. She was going to have to have a serious talk with Matt.

'It isn't that. You have the wrong idea. I –'

'Perhaps you don't know which ledger I mean?'

'I do. I'll get it for you,' she said.

'Thank you.'

Matt eyed his brother with lazy interest. 'Honestly, Zach, you're like a bear with a sore head this morning. What's eating at you? And what did you want to see me about, that was so important?'

Zach shot him a cool glance. 'The plans for the new pool and sun lounge, for one thing. We talked about it for long enough, so you can't have forgotten what we agreed, but I don't see any signs that you've done anything to set the ball rolling. It was some four months ago when we first discussed it, and I would have thought you had at least had the blueprints made up by now. I can't find them anywhere in the office, but perhaps you have them filed away somewhere else?'

'Ah.' Matt wandered over to the window and abstractedly ran his thumb over the sill. 'The pool. I meant to talk to you about that.'

Zach's dark gaze narrowed. 'I'm listening.'

Amber was feeling slightly numbed by this exchange. So, Matt had known all about Zach's plans from the beginning, but had done nothing about them, had said nothing... had let her go blindly ahead... But why? Because he wanted to please her?

Matt's shoulders lifted in a light shrug. 'You were away, and involved in something else, and I thought it wouldn't hurt to leave it for a while. Then we had this other idea -'

'Other idea?'

Sparks flickered in Zach's eyes. He looked at Amber as she held out the ledger, and she said quickly, 'Matt means me. I didn't know you had something else planned for the West side of the Park, and I thought it would be a great idea if we utilized some of the Park's existing habitat, and created a wild life area, with footpaths for people to walk along so that they could enjoy a kind of nature trail. I thought maybe we could bring in school parties, arrange guided tours and make more of the autumn and winter bookings.'

She wished she could tell what he was thinking. 'Picnic areas, too,' she went on. 'I thought they'd go down well... and then there was the pets' corner and...'

'Pets' corner?' Zach looked at her sharply. 'So that accounts for all the odd items of expenditure

Liza was telling me about.' He took the ledger from her. 'Just how long have you two been hatching this plan?'

Amber pushed at a wayward tendril of her hair that persisted in falling across her forehead. 'A few months, I suppose. It takes time to work out exactly what needs doing, how it should all be best laid out.'

'But you haven't actually started any of the work yet? I didn't see anything out of the ordinary when I looked around the other day. Of course, I haven't had time to see everything...'

'Some of it,' she admitted. 'Most of the planting was to be started in the autumn, and followed through in the spring, but the animals for the pets' corner have started coming in now. That's why I – we - were late this morning. There was a problem we had to deal with.'

His gaze wandered over her. 'With you involved, I can well imagine it. You had better come along with me and show me exactly what you've been doing, and what this problem was.'

Matt sauntered towards the door. 'You won't be needing me, then? I have one or two things I should be getting on with.'

'Like the blueprints for the pool and sun lounge,' Zach said, his cool tone stopping Matt mid-stride. 'We agreed on procedure, and I want costings made as soon as possible. Like, this week.'

Amber's teeth surreptitiously tugged at her lower lip. So, it was as she'd thought all along, and he wasn't going to let her go ahead and see her idea through to the end. It was hard to know which was worse, the shattering of all she had planned, or the guilt over the money she had already laid out in payments or on deposits. It would all have gone for nothing. And what was she to do with the animals? Would the suppliers take them back?

Matt was nodding cautiously and, clearly, he wasn't going to fill Zach in on the truth of the situation.

'And there was one other matter, before you slope off.' Zach picked up a couple of invoices and slid them across the desk towards him.

Matt glanced at them, reading the name of the garage at the top, and immediately began to lose some of his colour. 'Ah… yes. I was hoping you wouldn't find out about that,' he muttered. 'I thought I'd managed to bury the evidence.'

'Bury might well have been the operative word,' Zach said succinctly. 'It could have been you who finished up wound round the tree, and not just the car.'

Unsteadily, Matt asked, 'How did you find out?'

'I rang the garage.' Zach's gaze flickered over Amber, who swallowed hard. 'One or two things didn't quite ring true, and I wanted to know what was going on. The garage obligingly sent me copies of the invoices.'

'It was just high spirits, nothing more,' Matt said. 'I've learned my lesson, you know.'

'I should hope you have.' Zach's voice had a cutting edge. 'If it was high spirits that led to your smashing up two cars, you had better start cleaning up your act pretty fast, before somebody ends up in the hospital. Was Amber with you when these accidents happened?'

Matt shook his head, his expression sombre. 'No.'

'Then you can thank your lucky stars for that. If she'd been with you, and you'd risked her neck as well as your own, or anyone else's for that matter, I'd have thought seriously about withholding the next portion of your trust fund. As it is, you'd better make certain your driving record's as pure as driven snow from now on, otherwise you'll find yourself in deep trouble.'

Zach pushed the invoices into a briefcase, and snapped the lock closed. 'We'll talk some more, later. Right now, Amber and I have a few things to deal with.'

He dropped the briefcase on to the desk, then moved to the door and held it open. 'After you, Amber. You can show me just what it was that kept you out of the office first thing.'

'I thought you'd already made up your mind about that,' she said, as they walked out into the hot sunshine. She'd been right about the heat. It was going to be a scorcher. 'You thought Matt and I were together all night.'

'Was I wrong? Matt makes no secret of the fact that he lays claim to you.'

'No one has a claim on me,' she retorted.

His hard mouth twisted. 'You sound very fierce. Does that mean you don't sleep together, or that you prefer to keep an independent spirit?'

He sounded sceptical, and that annoyed her.

'It means,' she stated firmly, 'that what I do in my own time is my business. I don't enquire into your private life, and I don't see why you feel you have a right to know about mine.'

'I have a right, when I think it's interfering with your work,' he said coolly.

'And if it does that, I'll consider telling you about it.' She led the way to the meadow land that bordered one side of the lake. 'I suppose it's pointless discussing it now,' she said, 'but I thought this might be the start of the wild life trail, and then right over there, by the copse,' she gestured into the distance, 'would be ideal for a children's play area. You know the sort of thing, I'm sure, with logs and rope swings, tyres and tunnels, and so on.'

'That too?' he murmured. 'You have been busy these last weeks. And what about the pets' corner? How many acres was that meant to cover? I take it you were thinking on a grand scale, in keeping with the rest of your ideas?'

She wasn't sure whether he was annoyed with her, or intent on laying bare all the facts. His tone was even enough, but that could be deceptive. Zach Berkeley would make up his own mind what he wanted, and he wouldn't let her get in his way.

They had arrived at the area being penned off, a shady part of the Park where bushes and trees bordered a small pond. She was glad to see that the rabbits and guinea pigs at least were still safely housed. Perhaps he hadn't ventured this far, amongst the rural pathways when he'd looked around.

'I see I was right,' he murmured, looking around at the area of land that had been fenced off, with various enclosures. 'You were thinking big. What other animals are we expecting?'

She eyed him warily, uncertain about his reaction. 'A couple of donkeys are due to arrive sometime this afternoon.'

'I should have guessed,' he murmured, rolling his eyes. 'And are we to give donkey rides, too?'

'Only when they're fit enough. They've been rescued and need time to graze and build themselves up a bit. I thought they would go down well with the holiday makers who have young families,' she agreed, uneasily. 'And pony rides... with qualified instructors, of course.'

He leaned against the fence. 'Of course. No doubt there will be special feeding times, with keepers in attendance, and peacocks and poultry wandering about, and fresh laid eggs despatched at regular intervals to the restaurant.'

'Well, that had occurred to me -'

'I can see how this idea appeals to you,' Zach said, 'but we're not meant to be a zoo. Do we even have a licence?'

'Oh yes, I arranged it.'

'That's one thing to be thankful for.' Then, 'What on earth -' He broke off suddenly and swung round as something began tugging at his trouser leg.

'Oh no,' Amber said, setting eyes on the goat, and trying to ward him off. But the goat wasn't having any of it. 'It's Dusty. We tied him to a post this morning after he broke free from his pen, but he must have escaped again.' She looked at the dangling end of rope that trailed from the loop around his neck. 'He must have chewed his way through the rope.' He'd been thwarted once already today, and now a tasty piece of expensively tailored material was

110

too good a prospect to miss. She tried sliding her fingers under the rope that circled his neck. 'I think he must have taken your mention of feeding literally.'

'Dusty?' Zach and the goat were engaged in a tug of war. 'Isn't that an odd name for a goat?'

'It's short for dustbin,' she explained breathlessly, still playing tug of war with the rope. 'He eats anything, you see.'

'So I've gathered.' Pulling himself free, at last, he inspected the damp hem of his trousers and added ruefully, 'I think I'd prefer it, though, if he didn't get a liking for my suits.' He took the rope from her, and started to lead the reluctant animal purposefully towards one of the outbuildings. Amber picked her way carefully over the roughly gravelled path, trying to keep up with him.

'Your trousers aren't ruined, are they?' She looked anxiously at the hem of the one-time immaculate trousers, and Zach threw her a sideways glance.

'I dare say they'll be good as new once they've been dry-cleaned. But perhaps I should have taken out some kind of insurance before I came back to Lake View. Somehow, since I met up with you, I seem to be having more misadventures than average.'

He didn't stop to watch her dismayed expression. Dusty was unceremoniously bundled into a shed, much to the animal's annoyance, and the door was firmly bolted. 'I'll get someone over here to house him properly, while I decide what's to be done with him,' Zach said. 'Who's looking after these animals?' They moved away from the shed, making their way over the uneven ground.

She shifted uneasily. 'I am, for the moment,' she said. 'I won't let it get in the way of my work, though, not again. I had arranged for Dusty to be dealt with this morning, but things went wrong. We were going to set someone on to take care of the animals on a permanent basis, but then…'

'Then I came on the scene, and you had second thoughts, or Matt did, about the whole thing, and you didn't want another salary showing up in the accounts just yet. I take it that the goat was the cause of your difficulty this morning?'

She nodded, stunned by the accuracy of his summing up. 'It won't happen again.'

'No, it won't.' They started to walk back across the uneven ground towards the Admin centre. 'And you won't be using up all your free time in catering for a menagerie, either. I'd have thought you had enough to do, without taking that on, as well.'

'I don't mind, really I don't.'

He clasped her hand in his, drawing her close to him as she took measured steps across the gravel strewn footpath. She looked up at him, all too conscious of the way her soft, feminine curves were gently crushed against the hard length of his body. 'The path's rough,' he explained, 'and you're wearing high heeled shoes.' He stopped walking and slipped his arm around her waist, steadying her, and the intimacy, coming out of the blue like that, was sweetly compelling, shocking even. Her body hungrily absorbed all the new sensations that were flooding through her.

'You *should* mind about looking after them,' he said, and his smoky gaze was drifting over her, lingering on her face, her eyes, the smooth silkiness of her cheek, the soft outline of her mouth. '*I* mind.'

She stared at him, her lips parting, the breath catching in her chest. 'But it's no trouble,' she said, an odd huskiness about her voice. 'Not usually, anyway.' Held like this, she felt incredibly safe, protected, as though he had created a warm, inviolable circle just for the two of them. She'd never felt like this before... as though she'd come home. She didn't want to move. She wanted to stay here, locked in his arms for ever. 'I like animals – pets –' she said. 'They're innocent, affectionate... they're unconditionally loving... for the most part. They make me feel calm...'

'I guess that's something that's been missing in your life,' he murmured thickly, his hand flattening against the small of her back. 'Those things are important to you, and it follows that you bring those elements with you, into your work. You have some really good ideas, and you obviously have a great affection for animals but, the point is, you're not employed as a keeper.'

'No.' He held her so close that the word was muffled against his throat, her cheek brushing his skin. Pressured into the haven of his chest, she felt his warmth seep into her through his shirt, felt her breasts firm in tingling response. His hands shifted, moving over her spine, shaping her to him, and her heart began to thump heavily against her rib cage, her pulse racing violently out of control.

'You're a sweet girl, Amber. I could easily find myself becoming very attached to you.' His lips feathered along the line of her cheekbone, drifting over her face on a slow, lingering journey of discovery towards the soft fullness of her mouth. She looked at him, read the heated invitation in his smouldering glance, and all at once there was an answering fever in her blood, drawing her to him in a hot whirlpool of need. Her mouth tilted, touched his in hesitant exploration and then moved shyly away again, as the overwhelming temptation to cling shocked her to the core. He followed swiftly, swallowing up her retreat, claiming her mouth in heated possession. She closed her eyes, drinking in the pleasure of that kiss.

His mouth moved persuasively on hers, coaxing, caressing, tasting her sweetness, and her heart seemed to stop beating, the world and time stood still, and there was nothing else but this tide of longing. It consumed her, took her over and swept her away, tossing her on the crest of the wave; then cast her adrift as he slowly released her. 'You aren't meant to be with Matt,' he said. 'He isn't the one for you.'

She stared at him, too disorientated for words, her mind still flowing with the kiss, her eyes hot and intensely blue. 'Is that why you kissed me? To prove a point?'

'I'm just saying, you don't seem to be too sure about what you really want.'

She pulled in a breath. 'Perhaps that's because I'm not. My ex cheated on me after we'd been together for around eighteen months – he thought he could go on seeing another woman at the same time that he was telling me how much he loved me. He was only sorry because he was found out. I'd trusted him, but he let me down. I'm not likely to allow myself to fall head over heels for anyone else after that, am I? And, to be honest, I don't feel I can trust anyone to be there for me through thick and thin. Not even my family.'

He frowned. 'I guess not,' he said, his tone roughened. 'I can see how you would feel that way. And, actually, all this explains why you want to devote all your care and attention into looking after the animals. They reward you with affection and gratitude, regardless of what else is going on. It's sad, though, that you feel you can't rely on your family. Do you see much of them?'

'I do. I drop in on them most weekends to see how they're doing. Usually they're very busy, but we find time to have a meal together, or at least have a coffee. It's my birthday soon, though, and they said we would go away for the weekend, perhaps to my favourite seaside place in Devon, make it something special. They have a cottage there, close to the sea, and they promised we would all go over there.'

'That sounds good. It looks as though they're making an effort to do something just for you.'

'Yes, it does. I'll just wait and see if it actually happens.' She hoped it would come about, but quite often something managed to get in the way of any plans they made.

Zach frowned, then glanced around as the sound of voices drifted on the air. 'We'd better go. Someone's coming.'

Cautiously, she began to focus once more on her surroundings, her ears catching the soft sounds of an approach. Zach started to move away, taking her with him, his hand supporting her elbow as he led her over the difficult path.

Zach's tread was firm and sure footed, and while she was thankful for it at the moment, at the same time she knew a perverse disappointment that he had clearly not been as profoundly disturbed by their encounter as she had been. But then, why should he be? He was attracted to her, as he might be towards any woman with her fair share of feminine appeal, but it didn't mean anything. He was just behaving like a normally healthy, red-blooded male... as he might well have done with Liza last night... That unhappy thought made her stomach quiver convulsively. And maybe, just maybe, he was paying attention to her in order to keep her away from Matt. That notion shocked her. How could he do that? Would she ever find someone who would love her and care for her just for herself? Those were irrational thoughts, though. Didn't she know by now that she wasn't ever going to find everlasting love?

They had reached the lake side, and they stopped by a gnarled sycamore as Zach looked over to the reed fringed island in the distance. Amber carefully disengaged herself from his hand, aware of the flickering glance he gave her.

'I shouldn't have worn these shoes,' she said. 'If I'd known I wasn't going to stay in the office, I'd have worn something more sensible.'

Zach acknowledged that with a wry smile and returned to his contemplation of the island.

'It looks bigger than I remembered, and much greener,' he said. 'Perhaps it's just that the trees are spreading. The branches haven't been lopped in a while. They're long overdue for pruning. And some of those reeds could do with being thinned out.'

'Could they?' She sent him a faint, worried frown. 'I hope you won't do anything about it just yet - the ducks are hatching eggs. The wildfowl, too. It would be an awful shame to disturb them.'

'I wouldn't do that. Do you think I'm totally lacking in any moral sensibility?' His eyes had narrowed on her, and she looked away, not wanting him to read the uncertainty in her expression.

'I don't think I would have put it quite that strongly,' she muttered. 'I worry about what happens to them. I've spent a lot of time working out how my ideas for a wild life area and pets' corner can be fitted into the Park. I'm sure a lot of people would appreciate being able to enjoy the natural environment. I don't know what your feelings are on the subject… you haven't told me – except to say that you wanted to set up your pool and sun lounge near here.'

'If I haven't said anything it's because I'm still giving it some thought. 1 haven't made up my mind yet.'

'I see.' At least he hadn't thrown out the idea completely, then. 'I didn't mean to push,' she said. 'I'm sorry if all this has caused a hitch in your plans. I didn't know I was treading on any toes. It's just that the West side of the Park is so full of natural beauty with the lake and the island and it oozes rustic charm - it seems to lend itself to that kind of development, and I suppose I just got a bit carried away, talking to Matt about it, and the whole thing just grew. It all seemed so exciting at the time, and Matt… well, perhaps Matt was carried away, too, by my enthusiasm.'

'I can see how he might be.' His tone was dry, and she shot him a quick, searching look. 'You have a very persuasive way about you,' he went on. 'Enough to make any man lose his head, and Matt is a prime candidate for that, isn't he? He's so besotted with you, he doesn't seem to be able to keep his mind on anything else for more than two minutes. It's no wonder he's so ready to give you whatever you want.'

'It isn't true.' She was appalled that he could even think such a thing. 'He was as keen on the idea as I am. He didn't need any persuading.'

'Maybe so. But he should have cleared it with me first.'

'I don't know why he didn't do that, but perhaps he's conscious that he can't live up to your achievements, or be what you want him to be, and this was his way of showing you that he could cope without having to come to you with every decision. He must have thought you'd be pleased. In any event, I'm pretty sure he thought he had complete autonomy while you were away.' Her glance met his. 'Perhaps you could meet him half way... find out what really makes him tick – because I think he might be having doubts about whether he's cut out for the role you have in mind for him.'

'What makes you think that?'

'He hinted as much to me. I wonder if he's beginning to think that if he acts on his own initiative it might go all wrong. He can't live up to your expectations, so therefore he's giving up on trying. That way, he can't be accused of failing.'

'And where did that little gem come from? The Amber Kingston school of bizarre psychology?' He shook his head. 'I'm very fond of my brother, and he knows it. It's true we've been through a difficult patch just lately because he's let things slide, but I don't believe he's worried about my opinion, at all. He's just lost his way, and I want him to find it again, fast. He's intelligent and perfectly capable, and watching him drift off course is a painful experience. I've looked out for him all his life. His meandering has to come to an end at some point, and the crux of the matter is that while you're around, it won't. I don't believe your relationship with him is doing him any good, you're far too much of a distraction, and I think it would be for the best if you two parted company. I'm sorry if that hurts you, but that's how I feel. I don't believe you're the right woman for him. You said yourself your feelings don't go too deep after your experience with your ex.'

'Even so… I like Matt. I enjoy being with him, and I don't see why we can't be together and see where it takes us.' She stared at him. Did he really think so badly of her? His words stung and her throat ached with the knowledge that to him she was a mere amusement to be cast aside on a whim. She moistened her lips. 'Are you always so sure of yourself? What makes you think you can set yourself up as a judge of what's right for other people? Are you actually implying that I'm not good enough for your brother?'

'I didn't say that. I only know you'd do far better to turn your attention to me. Why were you so hungry for my kisses, if he means so much to you?'

119

His whiplash comment caught her on the raw, and she gasped, paling rapidly. Had those kisses meant nothing to him at all, except an experiment to see how quickly he could undermine her loyalties? Had he done it simply to prove that he could take her away from Matt? What was she to him, just a diversion?

'Hungry? Was I?' She injected some steel into her voice. 'Perhaps I was curious to see the expert at work. Your reputation has gone before you, didn't you know? You said yourself the Berkeley name attracts a lot of attention from women, but personally, I think it's very much overrated.' Her throat closed on the lie.

'Is that so? You're entitled, of course, to your opinion... but as to your response to me, I have to say you're either a liar, or a very fine actress.' His eyes glinted. 'It would be intriguing to find out which.'

A little pulse began to hammer jerkily in her throat. She had been shocked by her reactions to him. They were so unlike anything she'd ever experienced before, but it wouldn't do at all to have him discover the true extent of his effect on her. Surely it was nothing more than just a wildfire attraction? Could she be blamed for falling under his spell? He'd been sympathetic to her, understanding, thoughtful. He was a charismatic, powerful man, and even after this short time she was learning to respect him for his business acumen, for the way he'd singlehandedly taken on the family firm, and especially for the way he loved and supported his brother after their parents' demise.

Her thoughts veered away. He must never know how deeply she was attracted to him. It would be like placing a weapon in his hands, because once he knew just how frantically alive he made her feel, how just the merest touch of his hands could stir her sleeping senses, she would be completely at his mercy. He would take what she had to offer, and while she was tenderly nurturing her new-found emotions, he would be restlessly disentangling himself. She would never have any place in his world. He was a business man, first and foremost. He worked hard, and he played hard, and, sure as the sunrise, he would move on, out of her life and on to new business ventures, new loves.

'But you won't try to put it to the test,' she said huskily, 'not if your brother means as much to you as you say he does. You wouldn't want to hurt him.'

She had to force herself to accept the truth, that Zach Berkeley was never going to stay around to cherish a relationship. She had known that from the first, so where was the sense in falling for him? There was none at all. She would be hurt all over again. Why couldn't her foolish heart recognize the simple logic of that?

CHAPTER SIX

'THAT'S RIGHT. He's my brother,' Zach said, 'and I'll do whatever I have to do to protect him.' He checked his watch. 'We must head back to the office - I have a meeting with Rafael in just a few minutes.'

They walked across the compound in silence, Amber running her mind over his cryptic statement. What did he mean, he would do what was necessary? He wanted her out of Matt's life, he had made that clear enough, but what was he intending to do? Did he mean to fire her? She'd made a few mistakes but, surely, he couldn't dismiss her that easily? Or perhaps he had something else in mind?

She was glad of the air conditioning when they arrived back at the office. Her hair was faintly damp from the heat, and she went and stood by the fan for a while, letting cool air drift over her face.

Matt was just finishing a phone call, and Liza purred into action, pouring coffee for Zach and presenting him with a neatly typed batch of letters.

'Would you have time to sign these before you go off to your meeting? I'd like to get them in the post before lunch.'

'That was quick work.' He took them, skimming rapidly through each one before he reached for a pen.

'That's great,' Liza said, when he handed them back to her. 'I'll go and take these down to the post room right away.'

Matt took Amber to one side, and said, 'I hate to do this, but I'm going to have to cancel our date for this evening. A friend from University has arrived in town, and he wants me to go with him to look at some premises. Ted has it in his mind to start up a new restaurant. His father's putting up some of the money, and if he approves of the place, it's all systems go. I'd take you along, but Ted reckons it's not in the best condition at the moment. A lot needs doing to it, and it looks a bit like a builder's yard right now. You don't mind, do you?'

'Of course, I don't mind. You go ahead.'

She smiled at him and he squeezed her arm affectionately. 'I'll make it up to you.'

'You don't need to do that,' she said. 'Go off and enjoy yourself. I think you get a kick out of restaurants, don't you? Even if it's just talking about them... you're always taking me off to try out new ones.'

He mused over what she had said. 'You're right, I do have a thing about them. It's the food, of course, and the way each place is different, I think. Each one has its own special ambience. I envy Ted, in a way. It must give him a real buzz to be working on a design of his own, setting it up just as he wants it. He's thinking along French lines at the moment.'

'Wish him luck from me,' she said.

'Will do.' He picked up his jacket and hooked it over one shoulder, walking to the door. He gave Zach a nod of greeting along the way and said, 'I've fixed up a meeting with the architect. I'm on my way now. We'll start going over plans for the pool.'

'That's great. I'll see you when you get back,'

Amber went over to her desk and unlocked her drawer, taking out the memory stick she'd used the day before to save her work. Since the mishap with the translations, she was taking no chances.

Zach noticed, and his eyes gleamed faintly in acknowledgement. 'Would you deal with these for me?' he asked, sliding a pile of documents across the polished surface of the table. 'If you could manage to have them ready by tomorrow morning, I'd appreciate it. It will give Rafael time to check the details and get back to me with his comments.'

She scanned them quickly. 'I'll try. I've a lot to get through, but it should be possible, providing there are no interruptions. Is everything going well with the Spanish deal? No hiccups of any sort?'

'None, so far. It looks as though we should get everything signed before the week's out, and then in a few weeks' time I could be dealing with the rest of the negotiations in Spain.' He hesitated. 'I'd meant to talk to you about the plans for Lake View this morning, among other things, to see if we could figure something out, but it will have to wait, there isn't time now. Maybe we could do it this evening, if you have nothing already planned? I could come to your place, if that's okay with you?'

He couldn't have helped overhearing what Matt had said to her, cancelling their arrangement, and she answered quietly, 'After eight? I have a few odd jobs to get through before then.' She wondered what decision he might come to concerning the Park and about her role here. With Liza established in the Admin department she doubted there would be a place for her for much longer.

'Good, that's settled, then.' He gathered up his briefcase, and said, 'Don't look so anxious. I don't bite. At least, not often.' He gave her a sudden, brief smile, one that sparked dancing lights in his eyes and tugged attractively at the corners of his mouth. 'I'll bring some takeaway food, if you like, and a bottle of wine.'

'Okay. That'll be good.' She remembered what Matt had said, and tried to take heart. He might bite, and he didn't think she was innocent, but he had smiled at her, and she could live for a week on that smile, though it wouldn't do to read anything into it. 'I hope your meeting goes well.'

She worked steadily after he'd gone, cutting a swathe through the papers on her desk, and wondering if she could make time to shower and wash her hair, and change into something dreamily romantic, something that would knock him for six as soon as he set eyes on her.

A sigh hovered on her lips. It was all fantasy. She could never begin to compete with the women in his life. She was just a simple country girl at heart, and he... well, Matt had told her about the kind of women

Zach went for. Cool sophisticated, glamorous. Women like Liza. Women who knew the score, and would be content with an expensive pay off at the end, when he was ready to move on.

She didn't want to face the thought of his moving on, but it was bound to happen, and he'd said himself that his next port of call would probably be Spain. Zach never stayed in one place for more than a few weeks, or months, at most, and so far, she'd hardly made such an impact on him that he'd move heaven and earth to keep her by his side. That was just a fanciful dream, doomed from the start.

Determinedly, she concentrated on her work through the rest of the day. As soon as she finished here, she had the animals to feed, and she wanted to go over to the island and check on the ducklings that had recently hatched. The mother bird had injured her wing, and though she seemed to have been coping well enough with it up to now, Amber couldn't help worrying about her. She'd called the vet to check on her, and he'd immobilized the wing and said he would look at her again in a few days, but he wanted Amber to keep an eye on her in the meantime. She'd have to get a move on, but after she'd seen to everything she might just have time to get ready before Zach arrived.

'Would you check with the catering department before you go, today?' Liza asked, breaking the thread of her thoughts. 'There's a bit of a panic on. Some mislaid orders for supplies. Matt looked into it, but it's still not sorted. I can't see to it myself, I have to finish work on these new security arrangements. They are rather urgent.'

Amber couldn't help wondering why the security arrangements couldn't have waited, but it would probably be quicker if she went over to catering herself. She was familiar with the set-up there and she might be able to deal with the problem more easily than Liza.

Reluctantly, she put her own work to one side, and Liza said, 'I notice you haven't finished the translations Zach gave you this morning. Still, I dare say he won't mind waiting while you finish them off tomorrow.'

He wasn't going to have to wait, Amber thought grimly. She'd blotted her copy book enough since he'd arrived here, and she'd stay and finish them if it took her an hour or more of overtime. She wasn't telling Liza that, though, and she locked her drawer and went off to the catering department in a tenacious mood.

Liza had already left for home by the time she returned. Amber worked as fast as she could, but she was late leaving the office, and it meant she was going to have to hurry through her chores. She dashed back to the apartment for a change of shoes and a quick cup of coffee and then set off.

The heat hadn't dissipated as she headed for the feed store, and she wouldn't be surprised if there was a storm brewing. That worried her a little. The sky was getting ominously dark, and there was a stifling, oppressive quality to the atmosphere. She hurried through the feeding, and watering, and checked that the animals' bedding was dry and clean.

Dusty seemed to have recovered from his fit of the sulks and was too engrossed in exploring all the strange bits of wooden junk that had been strategically placed in his new pen to give her more than a cursory glance.

'You know who you have to thank for that, don't you?' she addressed him sternly. 'The boss has organized those playthings to keep you occupied. Ungrateful animal. It's more than you deserve.' Leaving him to it, she went off to sort out a boat to take her across to the island.

Most of the boats had been tied securely for the evening at the far reach of the water, by the pay kiosk, but she noticed that there was one moored on the lake, partly hidden by reeds and yellow water irises. That would do. It would save her having to go and hunt for the attendant, who was probably enjoying a well-earned rest by now. His shift finished an hour ago. In the morning, she'd tell him this one boat had been overlooked.

The motor was a bit sluggish, but after a few fits and starts it finally responded, and she cruised over to the island, stopping to tie up by a weathered wooden platform. Stepping off the planking on to the rough, brown earth, she wandered along the water's edge until she found the little family she was looking for, and delightedly discovered two new additions, soft with down, their tiny little webbed feet carefully padding over the grassy bank. Thankfully, the bandage was still intact on the mother's wing.

Throwing down a handful of feed pellets, Amber sat back on her heels and watched the parents and their offspring scoff eagerly until the first drops of rain began to fall. Thunder rumbled in the distance, and the anxious parents began to gather up their brood.

'I have to go now,' Amber whispered. 'You will keep them under cover, won't you? Shelter them from the storm?'

They seemed to know what to do, anyway, and she hurried back to the boat, alarmed by the way darkness had rapidly fallen, conscious of the thunder building to a roar overhead. Rain hissed around her as she struggled to start the motor, and she wished she'd taken the time to at least collect a jacket from the apartment. Already her blouse was soaked through.

The motor wouldn't start. No matter what she tried, nothing happened, and she looked around worriedly. There were no oars. What was she to do? She wasn't that good a swimmer, and it was some distance to the far shore. She tried her mobile phone, aiming to call someone, but from here she couldn't get a signal.

If Zach was here, he'd surely know what to do, but it was useless to let her mind wander along that avenue; no one was going to come by here tonight, least of all Zach. The place was closed up till tomorrow morning, and everyone with a scrap of intelligence would be tucked in somewhere cosy and warm.

All the same, she wished Zach would come; even if she had to stay out here in the open all night, it wouldn't matter a jot as long as he was with her, she'd feel safe with him, but of course, he wouldn't come. He'd be waiting for her, back at the apartment, and he'd think she'd let him down. He wouldn't come in search of a girl who had no more sense than to get herself stranded in the middle of a storm.

Water trickled off her hair and down her back, and she shivered, and started to move away from the bank towards the trees. There was a rough footpath ahead, and she made her way towards it until a crack of lightning split the heavens, and she froze for an instant before pressing herself into the cover of some overhanging branches.

Lightning filled her with a dread that she couldn't explain, even to herself. It woke in her all sorts of primeval fears, a feeling of mortal terror in the midst of the elemental battle raging over the earth. The rain poured from the skies. She heard a throbbing noise, a hum of sound in the distance, and she wondered if it was more thunder rumbling, but she couldn't be sure. Then the lightning cracked again and she closed her eyes, covering her face with her hands.

Now, listening to the storm raging all around her, she tried to calm down enough to think. There was a shelter of some sort on the island, a brick building that had been intended for storage, but the door was solid and she'd have her work cut out getting in there. There was a summer house, too, that had been locked up for as long as she could remember, but maybe she could break one of the windows to get in. If she could just get her legs to move and get her out of this place... Another crack of lightning rent the sky and she shrank back into her shelter, afraid to move.

There were sounds all around her, confusing sounds, rustlings and drips and the slashing beat of the rain as it hit the ground. They were hard to distinguish, one from the other, and then -

'There you are! Good heavens, Amber, I've been looking everywhere for you.'

The deep, masculine voice was like a balm to her senses. 'Zach?' Her heart gave a joyous, startled little leap, and she peered out through the mass of branches, her eyes growing rounder with every second. Her teeth were chattering, and she had trouble getting her words out. 'Wh… what are you doing here?'

'What do you mean, what am I doing here? When you weren't at your apartment and I couldn't find you anywhere on the Park I started to worry about you. Especially when the sky turned dark and it was clear a storm was threatening.' His tone was brittle, edged with concern. 'Why are you here? Don't you know any better than to hang about in the open in the middle of a storm? This is hardly the best of places to be when there's lightning around.'

'I hate lightning,' she said. 'I hate it.'

'I'm not surprised. No one wants to be out here in weather like this. Come out from under those branches.'

She stared at him, transfixed in a crouching position, feeling oddly tearful.

'I'm all right here. I'm sheltering.'

'Well, it isn't doing you much good,' he said firmly. 'You're soaked to the skin. Come on, let's get you out of here.'

She tried to untangle her limbs, feeling clumsy and awkward, and thoroughly miserable.

He bent down and reached for her hand, helping her up and taking her with him towards the footpath.

'Where are we going?' she asked.

'I thought we'd do best to head for the summerhouse,' he answered.

'I thought about trying to get to it, but then the lightning started.'

He made a wry smile. 'So, you clamped yourself to the nearest tree! Not a very good idea.'

'No, perhaps not,' she agreed, her words lost as he tugged her close to him and she buried her face in the fine material of his jacket.

Zach powered on through the undergrowth until he reached a clearing and the summerhouse came into view. He unhooked his keys from his belt, trying several until he found one that fitted the lock.

Amber chafed her damp arms with cold fingers, sniffing unhappily as he pushed open the door and ushered her inside.

'If I remember correctly, there should be an oil lamp in here,' he said, 'and a stove. Matt and I used to come here a lot when we were kids.' He produced a small torch from his jacket pocket and searched for a minute or two, shining the beam into the darkness. Then he found what he was looking for and applied a match to the wick. The flame burned brightly, lighting up the cabin, throwing long shadows into the corners.

Shivering, Amber pushed a hand through her dripping curls, and wiped the moisture from her face with the back of her hand. Her blouse and skirt clung to her, adding to her misery.

Zach said, 'Come over to the stove. It'll warm up in a minute or two.' He was already lighting the kindling as he spoke, then looked her over as she did as she was told. 'You ought to take off those wet things. There'll be a fleece throw in here somewhere.'

'I'll be all right, once the heater gets going.'

'Hm. I'm not so sure about that. You don't seem to be thinking logically at the moment, otherwise you wouldn't have come here with a storm brewing.'

'I know, but I thought I'd make it home in time. There was something wrong with the boat, otherwise I'd have been waiting for you at the apartment. I never meant to let you down. I'm sorry you had to go to the trouble of coming after me.'

'Don't worry about that.' He came to stand beside her, cupping her chin in his hand and tilting her head so that he could look into her eyes. 'I couldn't think what had happened to you. Then when the storm broke I started to worry, wondering where you were. I knew if you weren't there, waiting for me, there must be a good reason for it - and you hadn't left a message to say that there'd been a change of plan and that you'd gone off with Matt after all. The first thing I thought of was the animals. I went to check on them, and when you weren't anywhere around, I thought of this place. I saw a boat was missing and I had visions of you being adrift on the lake, or some such. I didn't know what to think.' He released her, making a wry face. 'Heaven alone knows why you wanted to come over here, but I felt sure this was where I'd find you. Aren't the eggs all hatched? Can't the birds fend for themselves?'

'Yes... I think they probably can,' she said, 'but the mother was injured a few days ago. I had the vet take a look at her, but even so...'

'You had to come and check.' His jaw tightened. 'I told you someone else was to see to them. That was an order, not a request.'

'But I feel responsible, and the vet asked me to keep an eye on her.'

'It's time to stop feeling responsible. I've already arranged for someone to take care of them. If you want to look to the welfare of any animals in this place, you can do it as an afterthought in your free time, not as an extension of your duties. You can't shoulder everything. No one can, and what you have to remember is that your responsibility begins and ends solely with the office. Matt should never have agreed to this project.'

There was a firmness about his tone that drove home to her an unhappy awareness of her limitations. She had gone too far, not just in her concern for the animals, but in dragging Matt along in the wake of her enthusiasm for everything else. She'd stepped over the unwritten line.

'I'll try to remember,' she mumbled. 'But I don't see how you can expect me to think of my job in terms of nine-to-five office work. I've always been full of ideas and I've been used to working on my own initiative, but now I don't know what to think, because everything has been turned upside down in the last few days.'

'Well, we can talk about that.'

She nodded. Her emotions were all over the place. At first, she had wanted only to make a good impression on Zach as her employer, so that he would realize how invaluable she was to him at work. But now other hopes had crept in and caught her unawares, and she didn't know how to cope with these new unsettling feelings. It couldn't be, could it, that she wanted to be invaluable to him, the man? She wanted him to care for her, to need her, the way she needed him. Surely that had to be a futile hope? A stinging dampness threatened her eyelids and she blinked hard, clutching her arms close to her body to stop a shiver.

'You're soaked through,' he said flatly, 'and you must be chilled to the bone. You ought to be getting out of those wet things.'

'No.' The word came out quickly, more sharply than she'd intended. There was no way she was going to undress in front of him, even if she'd fallen, fully clothed into the lake. 'I'm fine as I am.'

A tremor caught her out in the lie, and he sighed and took off his jacket, placing it around her shoulders. It was warm from his body heat, smelling faintly of musk and his own essential maleness. 'You're nothing of the sort,' he muttered thickly. 'And you'll never make a decent liar.' He wrapped the coat around her and then folded her to him, tugging her into the circle of his arms and gently drawing her head down against his chest. His breath feathered over her hair. 'What am I to do with you?' he asked huskily. 'You'll probably catch your death of pneumonia.'

'I'm sure I won't,' she mumbled. 'I'm never ill.' His hard strength was building her up, his protective arms making a buffer between her and the storm raging outside. A shaky sigh racked her body and he gathered her closer still, his fingers laced in the tumbling mass of her hair. Her cheek was pressed against the fine material of his shirt, so that she could feel the steady thud of his heart beat, and she wanted to cling to him, to lose herself in that warm refuge. She didn't think he would mind if she did that, but she might regret it afterwards. He was feeling sorry for her and he was offering her comfort, nothing more. She mustn't expect any more.

'I'll be all right, now,' she whispered. 'It's just that the lightning bothered me.'

'Is there any particular reason for that? Is it the noise or the fear of what might happen?'

'No, it isn't that. At least... I don't think so. I don't know...'

'Did something happen in the past to make you feel that way? Did your parents react badly to storms?'

She thought about it. 'No, not my parents, but Nico gets jumpy when lightning's around. Some years ago – it was an evening like this – he and I wandered off to play in the woods near where we lived. The day started off really hot, but it soon became oppressive and the sky was dark with rain clouds. The storm hit us when we were crossing a field, trying to get home, and we hid beneath an overgrown hedgerow. Nico was only nine years old and he was really scared of the thunder. I was too, but I hugged him and tried to tell him it was going to be all right. Apparently, everyone was frantic, trying to find us. Then Mum and Dad came along and took him from me. They wrapped him in a blanket and comforted him and I got a thorough telling-off for leading him astray. I was sort of left to trail behind them. It was only later when we were home and nearly an hour had passed that it dawned on them that I'd been frightened and soaked through too.'

'I'm sorry. That must have been a scary, unhappy situation, especially as you were both so young. So, it's not just the storm that bothers you, but the memory of being left out of your parents' affections?'

'I suppose so. I was older, though, going on thirteen, so I could take care of myself, but it was just one of lots of instances. I was afraid, frightened by the noise and the electric flashes, the way the whole sky seemed to light up.'

He stroked her arms lightly. 'You're safe now.'

'I know.'

'I could help you, you know… I could help you to find your real mother and then perhaps you'll be able to sort out some of the things that are giving you so much grief. It might be difficult, and it may not turn out the way you hope, but at least you'll have tried. Fear of the unknown is something that eats away at you and holds you back. Knowing about your past, and your background might help you come to terms with your emotions for once and for all.'

'Maybe. I'm just afraid she'll have a new family and she'll not want me.'

'The adoption agency might have a letter from her, something to say whether she wants to be contacted.'

'That's possible, I guess.'

He held her close, his hand in the small of her back drawing her to him. She wanted to stay wrapped up in his arms, but she knew she was treading on dangerous ground, and she ought to break away, now, before temptation got the better of her. He was comforting her, but he wasn't hers, was he? He and Liza were involved in some way, and she shouldn't read anything into this closeness. She shifted a little, stepping back, her fingertips pressing restlessly against his chest, until he covered her hand with his own and stilled her agitated movements.

'Stay,' he murmured, closing the space between them. 'You're cold. Let me warm you.'

She knew then, as he absorbed the soft friction of her curves against his hard frame, that she should ignore that husky invitation. She felt the tension in his muscles, the alert vitality of his lean body, and knew that she should be backing away; but all the time the reckless whisper of her senses was urging her to obey that soft voiced command, and stay exactly where she was.

'D - don't you think we should try to get away from the island?' she managed. There was a breathless quality to her voice, and she desperately tried to ignore the firm moulding of hip and thigh and the shock waves of awareness that were ravaging her self-control. 'The storm's easing off, isn't it, just a little?'

'No,' he said, his voice roughened, 'it isn't easing off at all.' His smoky gaze moved over her, heating her skin, and she had the feeling that he wasn't talking about the storm outside, at all.

'But we should get back, if we can. Anyway, you wanted to talk to me about work, about other things, you said. Perhaps we should concentrate on that.' She had to remember that he was her boss, keep her mind on course. It would be all too easy to delude herself into thinking that he might care for her. He didn't, he was attracted to her, nothing more. Breathing unevenly, she tried to draw away from him again, and the jacket slid from her shoulders to the floor. He moved with her, ignoring the jacket as he bound her to him.

'We can talk about work some other time,' he murmured, massaging her arms with hands that were surprisingly gentle, considering his strength. She felt the warmth beginning to seep into them. 'You've had a difficult time just lately, and right now, I suspect you're suffering a bit from shock. Just relax. Let me take care of things. You don't need to worry about anything.'

'But y-'

She didn't get to finish her protest. His head bent and his mouth captured hers, effectively silencing her, and then, when he began to brush his lips warmly over the softness of hers, it was the tenderness that was her undoing, the gentle, coaxing invitation in the slow, sweet drift of his tongue. Slowly, her resistance ebbed away, and nothing existed for her except this heady delight. His lips enticed her, playfully teased and tantalised, and a hectic thrill of excitement coursed through her, robbing her of breath and turning her insides to flame.

'You smell of soap, and baby oil,' he said huskily, 'and wild heather. I like that. I think I could get addicted to the taste and smell of you.'

The words brought her to her senses. It was a purely physical thing with him, whereas she... she could easily be carried away on a dream of what might be... 'I need you to stop, Zach,' she said. 'I can't do this. I can't keep stepping on and off this merry-go-round. You're my boss and we're never going to be together, you and me. It's just a flirtation, a light-hearted fling to you.'

His mouth made a wry twist of self-deprecation. 'I've wanted you since I first set eyes on you, and that hasn't changed. Heaven help me, even knowing that Matt is crazy about you doesn't do anything to change that. I've dreamed about having you, in my arms, in my bed, in any way there is. I can't get enough of you, but tell me how I reconcile that with my brother and my conscience?'

She heard the undercurrent of self-recrimination in his voice and bit down on her lower lip. 'I can't. You have to deal with that for yourself. More to the point,' she said, 'how are you going to tell Liza that you've been kissing another woman? You are having a relationship with her, aren't you?'

His mouth made a flat line. 'Not exactly. There *was* something between us, but it was never meant to be anything permanent.'

'I wonder if she realizes that?' Inside, she felt empty and upset. Relationships meant nothing to Zach. He had swept into her life with all the force of a typhoon, and soon he would just as quickly sweep out again, leaving her behind him, devastated. 'But that's how you are with women, isn't it, Zach? You want me, for fun, for pleasure, but not as part of anything long term, isn't that right? No one woman will ever have a lasting place in your life, will she, Zach? You take what's on offer, and then move on, isn't that the truth of it?'

His face was guarded. 'Is that what Matt told you?'

She nodded slowly. 'You said as much to me yourself. You said you steered clear of entanglements and didn't get too deeply involved. Your problem is that you don't dare trust anyone with your feelings.'

'I suppose that's the truth of it,' he said simply. 'I've learned to be cautious. At the same time, I can't offer a woman stability. I've spent the last ten years building up this Company. Work is what I thrive on. It's kept me going, it's been my life, and I'm always on the move because of it. I've never held out the promise of permanency to anyone, because I've never wanted to have my life mapped out a certain way. I've always had to be ready to change course on an instant, and there's never been any reason for me to discard that way of going on. If you were looking to me for anything more settled than that, you would be disappointed.'

She swallowed against the swollen ache in her throat. 'You're honest, at least.' She had already worked out for herself the way things stood, but his underlining it didn't make her feel any better.

'At least.' He gave a brief smile that had no trace of humour in it. 'You could share what I have to give, without taking it too seriously. That's the best offer I can make at the moment.'

Did he think he was laying the world at her feet? Any treasure was only hers to borrow. A tremor ran along her spine and she breathed in raggedly.

'Keep it,' she said. 'I've had enough of being second best. At least Matt cares wholeheartedly for me.'

A muscle flicked along the line of his jaw. 'I'm sorry you feel that way. I care for you, too, Amber. You've somehow managed to work your way into my psyche when I was least expecting it.' He sighed. 'At least you've dried out a bit with the heat from the stove, but I think we should make tracks for home. It sounds as though the storm's died down a bit, and maybe we should start back before it gets too dark to see out there. I don't think it would be a good idea to spend the night here. There's no food or water, and you need to get into some dry clothes.'

'Yes,' she said quietly.

He picked up his jacket and wrapped it around her once more. The simple, thoughtful gesture tore at the edges of her composure and brought the sharp sting of tears to her eyes. She fought them back fiercely, because she didn't want him to see. If she'd taken him up on his offer, he would have been kind to her, and tender, and more than anything in the world she wanted him to cherish her, but not for just a few weeks or months while he was in town. He would take her heart with him when he left, and she didn't think she could bear to watch him go.

CHAPTER SEVEN

NICO PHONED Amber next morning as she was getting ready to leave for work. 'Hey, Sis,' he said in his usual buoyant manner. 'How are things with you?'

'Just great,' she said. 'And you? Now that the exams are behind you, I bet you're feeling good knowing that you have several weeks of freedom ahead of you.'

'Yes, you're right. I'm going to spend time with friends, getting out and about.'

'That's the spirit!' It was good to hear his voice, and they talked for a while longer, sharing news about what they'd been doing. As they drew the conversation to a close a few minutes later, she said, 'I'll see you this weekend, won't I? I'm looking forward to staying at the cottage in Devon. It'll be like old times, walking on the beach, buying cockles from the seaside kiosks.'

'Ah… I need to talk to you about that, Amber.' Something in his tone immediately alerted her that something was wrong. 'Mum and Dad are going to call you later, when you finish work, but I thought you ought to be prepared. I know how much you were looking forward to the trip.'

'What's happened? Has it been cancelled? Is somebody ill?'

'No one's ill. It's just that a business opportunity turned up and they have to go over to Spain to check it out. After that, they're planning on spending a few weeks at the olive grove with Nan and Grandad. I'm sorry, Amber.'

She sighed, and tried to mask her disappointment. 'It's okay, Nico. It's not your fault.' She was reeling from the news, but she didn't want to let her brother see how badly it had affected her. 'I'll find plenty to do this weekend, don't worry. I take it you're going with them?'

'Yes, they'll drop me off at the olive grove, and I'm going to meet up with friends over there.'

'Well, have a good time. I'll see you when you get back.'

'See you, Sis. Take care.'

She felt numb with the alteration to her birthday plans, but she went along to Reception to deal with a problem that had come up, and then she set off for the Admin block. It was well after nine when she walked into the office, and Zach was already there, sifting through some paperwork. As soon as she saw him, a peculiar warmth suffused her, and her heart jumped a beat. She steadied herself by putting the large carrier bag she was holding on to the work top at the side of the room.

Zach looked lean and fit, and fully charged, and it didn't seem fair, when she was still feeling the lack-lustre effects of a disturbed, dream-filled night. She noticed that Liza and Matt were nowhere to be seen, and that was odd, but maybe they were busy on other things.

'I'm not really late,' she said. 'I had to deal with a problem in Reception on my way over here.'

'I wondered if you'd decided to sleep in,' he murmured, shooting a quick head to toe glance over her. 'I wouldn't have blamed you. You looked tired and thoroughly chilled yesterday, as though you needed to soak in a hot bath. Have you recovered – there've been no after effects?'

'Of course. I'm fine.'

He looked at her thoughtfully, and she hoped fervently that the light dusting of make-up she'd applied had been enough to disguise the faint shadows under her eyes. He was too sharp by half. She'd been careful over her dress, too, choosing a simple blue and white print because it looked fresh and summery, and with a bit of luck it might throw him off track. The last thing she needed in her present precarious mood was for him to know that she'd lost sleep over him.

'Are you sure you're feeling all right? You don't seem quite your usual self.'

'I've just heard from my brother that my birthday weekend has been cancelled.'

He frowned. 'I'm sorry. What happened?'

Briefly, she told him about her parents' business trip. 'It can't be helped, I suppose.'

'Couldn't they have arranged it for some other time?'

She shrugged. 'Apparently not. I guess I'll have to find some other way to celebrate.'

'It must be upsetting, a real let-down for you. Perhaps it's time to tackle some of these problems, once and for all. I get the feeling that your adoptive family is unlikely to support you come what may, but it doesn't mean that your real family don't want to be there for you. Don't you owe it to yourself to find out?'

'Maybe. But I don't know if my real mother wants anything to do with me.'

'You could find out. Then that would be one less hurdle to jump. You'd know, one way or the other.'

'Yes, you're right. Perhaps I ought to pluck up the courage to find out.' She felt uncomfortable talking about it. 'Isn't Matt around?' she asked, changing the subject to divert his attention.

His eyes narrowed as though he recognized her tactics. 'No, he isn't. He's hungover and he'll be in later when he's doused the effects of last night's binge with coffee.'

'A binge?' she echoed. 'That sounds as though he had something to celebrate. Perhaps his friend decided to go ahead with his plans to buy the restaurant.'

'Possibly.'

'You sound very non-committal,' she said, picking up on something in his tone. 'Didn't you speak to him this morning? Didn't he give you some idea of how things went?'

'I spoke to him late last night, but he wasn't forthcoming about Ted. I'd say he has a lot of things on his mind right now, a few options of his own to think over.'

She wasn't sure that she liked the sound of that, and she wondered what Zach had been saying to him. 'What kind of options? You haven't argued, have you? I wouldn't want -'

'I put a proposition to him,' he said dismissively. 'I expect he'll tell you about it himself when he's ready.' He moved over to the worktop at the side of the room and she knew with a sense of increasing frustration that he wasn't going to be forthcoming any more. 'What's in the bag?' he asked, changing the subject and letting his glance wander over the carrier bag she'd placed on the smooth surface.

Uncomfortably, she said, 'I brought your jacket with me, since you wouldn't take it last night. I'll take it to the dry cleaners. I hope they'll be able to get it back into pristine condition. It looks very rumpled, and I think -' she'd been about to say they must have trodden on it, but that brought back too vivid a reminder of that kiss in the summerhouse, and she changed it quickly to, 'the damp can't have done it much good,'

His glinting amusement told her he knew very well what she'd been thinking, but he refrained from comment as he took a look inside the bag. Tossing the carrier bag on to her desk, he said, 'I'll see to it.' His glance went to the hanger on the far wall, where he had placed his grey suit jacket earlier that morning. 'Luckily I have a spare. The airline returned my luggage this morning.'

'Oh, that's good. I'm glad. You must be pleased.'

'I am.'

She glanced at the pile of letters in her in-tray. 'I'd better make a start on the post.' Letting her attention wander to Liza's desk, she said, 'Isn't Liza coming in to the office this morning?'

'She's gone into town on an errand for me. She'll be back in an hour or so.'   'Oh, I see.'

'Do you? I wanted the office to ourselves, so that I could talk to you.' He stood up and came over to her.

'Is it about my work? Have I done something wrong? I know things have been falling apart lately, with work going missing and so on.'

'No, nothing at all like that,' he said firmly. 'In fact, you've worked calmly and steadily through all the things that have come your way. And as for things falling apart, it simply isn't true. You've coped well with everything that's been thrown at you, and even when things seemed at their worst, you didn't collapse in a heap or throw a fit of hysterics.' He paused, then said, 'Are you worried about the work I asked you to do yesterday? It doesn't matter that you didn't get it finished. You warned me that you had a lot to do, and I should have given you more time.'

She glanced at him, frowning. 'You mean the papers you gave me? What makes you think they aren't finished?'

'Liza pointed it out to me this morning. She said you probably hadn't managed to get around to them.'

Amber's chin lifted a fraction at that.   'Did she say why that might be?'

He shrugged. 'She mentioned that you had a back-log of work to get through.'

'There is a lot of work,' she admitted. 'It's always the same this time of year at the height of the holiday season, but the main difficulty yesterday was that a problem suddenly came up in the catering department. It took me some time to sort it out, but I did manage to do your translations when I got back to the office. They're in my desk.'

She went over to her table and unlocked the drawer, pushing the papers across to him.

He looked surprised, but gave her a warm smile. 'Thank you. I hadn't intended for you to work overtime. I know you have your routine work to see to.' He weighed the papers in his hands. 'It's very useful to have these, though. I'm meeting with Rafael in a few minutes and I'll pass them on to him. He'll be pleased to have time to study them before he leaves for Spain.'

'Is he leaving soon?'

'On Saturday. I'm organizing a small get-together at a hotel in town on Friday evening, so that we can celebrate the signing of our deal. I'm also inviting the staff from Lake View to thank them for all their hard work over the last year. We've had really good reviews and trade is well up on previous years. I'd like you to be there, Amber. Rafael will be pleased to see you before he goes home.' He frowned as he watched her drop the key to the drawer back into her bag. 'Is this business with the locked drawer a hangover from the translations that were mislaid a few days ago?'

'That's right,' she said quietly. 'I don't want to take any risks.'

'And you're concerned that something else might go astray? Do you think someone might have helped in some way to bring about their disappearing act?'

'I wouldn't like to say,' she told him cautiously. 'I've no idea what happened to them.'

Zach sat on the edge of the desk and sent a raking glance around the room. 'You're probably being discreet in saying that, but I'm beginning to get an inkling of what's actually going on here. You'll probably find them tucked away in an obscure part of the filing cabinet.'

'I didn't file them away.'

'No,' he agreed. 'But someone else might have. It's odd, isn't it, how a few small incidents have conspired to make it seen as though you're either inefficient or not up to the job?'

Her skin prickled. He was voicing her suspicions with such clarity that she stared at him in shock. 'It has seemed that way, hasn't it?' she said uneasily. 'I'm not usually inefficient, though. I work to the best of my ability, and I don't mislay things, at least, nothing of importance. And I'm not usually late without good reason.'

He nodded. 'I wouldn't have known that, of course, coming here and observing the way things have gone this last week. But I do know that you're well organized and conscientious. That's why things have been running so smoothly over the last few months, and that's how Liza was able to produce the costings I asked for at barely a moment's notice.' He stared broodingly at the neatly stacked files on the shelves around the room. 'I also know that Liza is desperate to have the overall management of this office. A good salary goes with the job, and she needs that, if she's to stay down here and be near her parents. He paused. 'Do you understand what I'm saying?'

'I think so.' Had he really worked out what had been going on? She had been anxious, unhappy about the way things had been going, and she'd been unwilling to give her suspicions any validity, but he, it seemed, had no such qualms.

'I've never known Liza behave like this,' he said, 'and I shall talk to her about it and get it all ironed out. I am sure, though, that she has no grudge against you personally. It's just that this is terribly important to her… and she is exceptionally good at her job.'

She felt her spine stiffen at something in his tone. 'What you're really saying is that you're going to offer it to her, in spite of what you think she's been doing.' She looked into his eyes and knew that she was right, and the anger of frustration and bitter disappointment ran through her in a hot wave. 'The fact that it's important to me, too, doesn't come into it.'

'It does, of course it does,' he murmured consolingly. 'Amber, believe me, I know what this means to you. I know you've all the qualities necessary to carry the job through. You're ambitious, and you've worked hard, and I'm well aware of everything that you've done here, but for the moment I'm asking you to bear with me on this. Your role here will change, and we need to think about exactly what that will be. There's a lot going on at the moment, so I'd rather we talked about it later, when we have more time and the surroundings are a little more… conducive.'

Conducive to what, she wondered, and she might have voiced her doubts, only he went on, 'After the party on Friday, perhaps? In the meantime,

Liza will need your support, and I'm hoping you'll try to accept the way things are, just for a while. Will you do that for me?'

Her whole body stiffened and she held her spine ramrod straight. 'I can't answer that now, I have to think things through.' Pride dictated that she didn't let him see how badly she was shaken by his decision. She had guessed, from the moment Liza had arrived, that this was the way things would go, but it didn't help to finally acknowledge that her dream was fading into oblivion. 'I don't know if I can work with Liza, show her the ropes and then take a back seat. You're asking too much of me.'

The door to the office opened with a clatter, startling them both. They turned to see Matt walk in, wincing as the noise rattled round his head, and trying to juggle a briefcase in one hand and rolls of documents in the other. He deposited them all thankfully on Amber's desk, then looked from one to the other.

'Am I interrupting something?' he asked. 'If you don't mind my saying so, the atmosphere in here seems a little tense.'

'We were discussing Liza's future role in the office,' Zach told him.

Amber noticed that he didn't make any reference to *her* future. What future did she have?

'That must mean you intend to promote her,' Matt accurately guessed. 'It was on the cards all along, I suppose. You've been doing a lot of sorting out in your head just lately, haven't you, Zach? Including mulling over what to do about me.' He gave his brother a considering stare. 'Well, you certainly sent me away with something to think about last night.' Glancing at Amber, he said, 'Did he tell you about it?'

She shook her head. 'Only that he'd made you a proposition of some sort.'

Matt walked over to where the coffee pot simmered gently and poured himself a cup. 'He's done that all right. He's certainly given me something to think about. He's suggested that I tour all the sites where we have leisure interests; that means throughout the UK and abroad. I'm to have a free hand to update the catering facilities, set up or re-design restaurants, cafés, grill rooms... do whatever I think best.' He studied her face over the rim of his cup. 'Clever, isn't he, my brother? It's an opportunity I might only have dreamed of, and now he's handed it to me on a plate. Somehow, I can't help wondering why. '

Zach said smoothly, 'Did you think about it?'

'I'd have to, wouldn't I? Only a fool would throw over a chance like that without giving it some serious thought. I talked it over with Ted. He thought it was a great idea. Sarah thought it was worth cracking a bottle over, too.'

'I thought she might.'

'Sarah?' Amber put in the soft query.

'Ted's sister. Zach knows her.' He placed his half empty coffee cup on her desk. 'She worked in his office in London, one time. Now she temps. She says it gives her more freedom from routine.'

'I suppose it would. Did the wine help you to come to a decision?'

'Not exactly. I wanted to talk to you about it before I made up my mind one way or the other, because my decision really depends on you. If I go, I'd like you to come along as my personal assistant. I think you'd get a lot out of it. It means staying in lots of new places, having your own say in what's to be done.' He smiled at her, his expression warm and inviting. 'I'd like you to come with me, Amber. Say that you will.'

She didn't know how to respond to his persuasive tone. The way things were going, there was little for her here, if Liza was to take over, and Zach... before too long, Zach would be going on his way, too, and her life would be empty like a barren desert. Yet how could she go with Matt, when he might be asking her for all the wrong reasons? He had always expected more of their relationship than she could give.

She said carefully, 'It sounds wonderful - just the sort of thing you've been looking for, with all that travel and challenge. You've never really settled here, have you? Oh, I know you've made the best of it, but I always felt that you were restless the whole time. I think you should go.'

'Only if you come with me.'

'It isn't that simple, Matt. You shouldn't base your decisions around me. I'd like to go with you, but -'

'Then you shall. It's all settled.'

'Matt, I th -'

Her words were cut off as Zach said sharply, 'She won't be going anywhere with you, Matt. She already has a job here.' Amber's head was beginning to throb.

'But not necessarily the one that she wants,' Matt threw back at his brother. 'You'll sort out this office to your own satisfaction before you leave for pastures new, and I know you well enough to be sure you must have some place in your grand scheme already worked out for Amber. I don't think she'll fall in with your plans, though. She's too sensible to jump in with both feet, and I think she'll turn her back on whatever you have in mind and go with me. I can give her everything she wants, you see.'

'Aren't you forgetting something?' Zach said tersely. 'A little matter of the contract she signed?'

'Contracts can be broken,' Matt said dismissively.

Amber didn't at all like the way this conversation was going. They were ignoring her completely, totally oblivious to what her opinion was. Instead, they were glowering at each other like baited bulls, ready to lock horns.

'Not this one,' Zach persisted. 'Not any contract I'm involved with. It still has some months to run, and it's binding to the last letter.'

Matt shrugged. 'So, we'll rearrange the lettering. I want Amber with me.'

Frowning, Amber said quickly, 'Matt, don't you think we need to -'

'Leave it to me, sweetheart,' he murmured, cutting across her attempts at resistance. 'I'll deal with everything.'

Her blue eyes narrowed as her mood became more fractious. He might almost have added, 'Don't bother your pretty little head,' his manner was so casually patronizing.

Zach's dark stare was dangerously honed. 'You won't find that as easy as you imagine,' he said with a harsh rasp. 'The offer was open to you, not Amber. You're quite right, I have my own plans for Amber, and she stays here.'

Amber's warring emotions had been heating up throughout this exchange, and now they were fizzing with barely repressed outrage. The day had started off badly with the cancellation of her weekend trip, which had reminded her all too clearly how little she could rely on her family – and maybe showed how low she came in their priorities; and Liza's machinations, aiming to paint her in a bad light to Zach, had irked her too. Then she'd lost all chance of the job she had coveted for the last year. Now, having Zach and Matt decide her future between them and treat her as though she wasn't there was the last straw. She had been ignored long enough, and if she didn't say her piece soon, she would explode.

Seething, she planted her hands firmly on the table in front of her and said through her teeth, 'Have you two quite finished discussing my options as though I wasn't here? You Berkeley men seem to think you can order people's lives about just as you please, and it's high time you learned otherwise. For your information - and this is for both of you to digest – *I* shall decide what I'm going to do with my life. I shall take time to think things through, and when I've made up my mind what I want to do about it, then I'll let you know. I may decide to leave and find work somewhere else.' Her mouth set grimly. 'In the meantime, this office doesn't run itself, and I have work to get on with, even if neither of you have. I'll thank you to clear your things off my desk and allow me to get on with it.'

She glared at both men. 'Well?' When neither of them made a move to do anything more than stare at her in astonished silence, she swept her arm in a wide arc which tipped both the carrier bag and the briefcase on to the floor. Then she dragged her chair savagely into position and sat down.

Matt eyed her with wary alarm. 'Amber… sweetheart,' he said, 'you shouldn't upset yourself this way.'

'Don't sweetheart me,' she muttered. 'You could try moving your papers out of my way.' She waved a hand over the rolled-up documents that were on her desk, giving him a questioning look, and when he still didn't clear them away she sent them to join the other things on the floor, making an untidy heap.

'Careful with those,' he implored. 'They're my plans for the pool and -' Several more documents followed, and he stared at her, his jaw dropping in dismay. 'Amber, darling girl -' Her fingers moved to the handle of his coffee cup that rested on the corner of her table and this time he picked it up and smartly backed away out of the line of fire. 'I'm sorry,' he said quickly. 'You let me know whatever you decide. Take all the time you need.' He began to nervously gather up his things from the floor, heading in an uneasy backwards zig-zag towards the outer door. 'I'll be in the other office if I'm needed. Just shout. Or give me a buzz.'

Her teeth gritted fiercely. Too irritable to speak, she snatched up the morning's post and ripped open the first envelope with a single slice of the letter knife.

Zach strolled over to the far side of the room and lifted his suit jacket from its hanger. Coming back to her desk he casually dropped it on to the polished surface.

'Go ahead, do your worst, while you're in the mood,' he said, his gaze shifting over the blade of the knife. 'You might as well fill today's quota here and now, and then I can go ahead and work out what's left in the wardrobe for the rest of the week.'

'Don't tempt me!'

He laughed softly. 'Oh, but I shall. Believe me, if there's any way I can tempt you, my angel, I surely will...' His low drawl wound its way seductively around her nervous system, undermining the flash of anger that had ruffled her feelings, and she fought a hard battle against it. 'What are you waiting for?' he murmured, watching uncertainty cloud her eyes. 'I dare say I could get used to living in jeans and tee shirts...'

'Oh! You're impossible,' she said. 'Don't you have work to do? Preferably somewhere else.'

He smiled, a crooked twist of a smile. 'I do, unfortunately,' he murmured, 'and yes, I need to be somewhere else. But I'll be free in a couple of hours. Why don't we take a long lunch break today, and drive over to Smugglers' Cove? It's a beautiful day, perfect for being on the beach. I think you need some time away from the office, so that maybe you can relax and get your head around some of the things that have been upsetting you today. We could talk things through.'

His suggestion took the wind out of her sails. 'We could talk about my job… about whether there's still a role for me, here?'

'Yes, that too.'

The more she thought about a trip out, the more the idea appealed. 'I think I would like to go to the beach. Thank you.'

'That's good.' He smiled his satisfaction. 'I'll come and find you – see you later.'

Amber changed into a pair of low-heeled shoes that she kept in the office, and refreshed her lipstick just before Zach came to pick her up at lunchtime. 'Do we need to take anything with us?' she asked him. 'Bottled water? Sandwiches from the cafeteria?'

'Nothing at all. I have it all in hand – I asked the catering department to organize a hamper for us. I wasn't sure what you liked to eat, so I made a fairly wide selection.' He smiled, his gaze skimming her slender figure. 'You look lovely - very summery in that pretty dress.'

'Thanks.'

He walked alongside her out to his car and opened the door to the passenger side so that she could settle comfortably. The air conditioning made the interior cool, a calming relief from the heat of the day, and the soft music coming from the radio was infinitely soothing. They reached their destination in just a few minutes, and Amber stepped out on to the tarmac of the parking place and looked towards the shimmering sea and the magnificent landscape. The sky was intensely blue. She saw a golden, sandy beach, with high cliffs and jagged rocks forming the backcloth of the bay. It was breathtaking. Narrow inlets gave access to the numerous caves and there was a rugged footpath near where they were parked, leading down to the beach.

Zach opened the boot of the car and took out a picnic blanket and a wicker hamper. Then he took her hand in his and helped her down the steep path to the cove below. 'Shall we sit here, in the shade of the cliff?' he said, pointing out a warm, sun dappled area of smooth sand. There were small shrubs growing out of crevices in the rock, providing greenery and shelter from the fierce rays of the sun.

'Yes, this looks fine.'

He laid out the blanket and she sat down, watching as he undid the clasp of the hamper and opened it up.

'Oh, wow!' she exclaimed. 'When you said you made a wide selection, you meant it!'

He laughed. 'Well, I thought you might like to sample a little of everything. There's a watermelon fruit salad for starters, or you could have cracker biscuits and pâté if you like.'

'Oh, I'll start with the fruit salad, I think. I'm really thirsty.'

'Okay, here you go. I'll pour you a drink – would you like low alcohol sparkling wine, or chilled fruit juice?'

'Fruit juice, please. Maybe I'll have wine later.'

They sat and ate, looking out over the sea as they tucked into sandwiches of chicken and chutney, ham and salad, and nibbled on sausage rolls, crackers and dips.

'I used to come here with Matt when he was a teenager,' Zach said. 'We'd climb the rocks and explore the caves and think about the men who'd been here before us a couple of centuries ago. I suppose if you've lived here all your life you know about the smugglers who used to bring their spices, tea, spirits and so on, on to the beach in the dead of night.'

She nodded. 'They'd hide it all in the larger caves, far back, where it was concealed from the Revenue men. It must have been a risky business but, apparently, they often had men with swords and pistols to protect them. I heard that in one place a tunnel had been dug to connect a cave with the local alehouse.'

'Sounds like a good idea!' He offered her a punnet of strawberries and she helped herself, savouring the sweet taste on her tongue.

'Mm, lovely,' she said. 'This reminds me of cream teas in our holiday cottage in Devon. There were strawberries grown in a barrel in the garden, and we'd pick them fresh for tea, and in September there would be raspberries ripening on the canes, and blackberries for apple and blackberry pie.'

'Home made? Does your mother like cooking?'

'She does, when she has the time. She showed me how to bake tarts and pies, so it's something I like to do when I get the chance.'

'That's something I really miss.' His expression was sombre for a moment. 'My mother used to love baking, and cooking wholesome meals. I remember the steamed apple puddings she made, and the delicious lamb casseroles.'

'Oh, I could make dinner for you one day, if you like,' she suggested. 'I can't promise it would match up to your mother's expertise, but it would certainly be home cooking.'

He smiled, his gaze drifting over her. 'That's a really generous offer. Thank you. I'd like that.' He studied her as she sipped a glass of wine. 'Have you thought any more about trying to find your birth mother? Only, this morning, when we spoke, it seemed to me that you might be more inclined to look into it.'

She swallowed the rest of her wine, enjoying the prickle of bubbles at the back of her throat. Putting her glass down, she said, 'Yes, I could do that. What do I have to lose? Things have been falling apart all around me, so they can't get much worse, can they?'

'They could get better.' He hesitated. 'Actually, Amber, I took the liberty of ringing the Adoption agency this morning. I hope you don't mind? I spoke to a woman there and, as you might expect, she wasn't allowed to give me any details, but she looked things up and she did say it might be worth your while to pay them a visit.'

'Oh!' She gave a small gasp. 'You did that? That was… I didn't imagine…' She frowned. 'If she said it might be worth my while - does this mean that my mother left a contact number, do you think?'

He nodded. 'I think that's probably the case. That's the reason I wanted to talk to you. I made a tentative appointment for you to see the woman from the agency tomorrow morning. If you like, I could take you over there – I imagine you might want some moral support, but I could wait outside if that's what you'd prefer.'

'I… it's a lot to take in… tomorrow morning… so soon.' Seeing her indecision, Zach poured her a glass of wine and she sipped it, giving herself time to think. 'All right,' she said at last. 'Yes, okay, I'll do it. Thanks, I think I'll feel better if you could go with me.'

'Tomorrow, then. Don't bother coming into work in the morning. I'll pick you up from your apartment at ten o'clock.'

'Okay.' It occurred to her that being out of the office would give Liza the opportunity to flex her muscles as the new Admin Manager, and perhaps Zach was aware of that, too. She didn't really want to be there to see it, and what was her role now anyway? Did she even have a job title? But she wasn't ready to ask him about that. Right now, as they cleared away their picnic and wandered along the beach by the water's edge, she could only think about the appointment at the agency and what it might reveal. She would worry about whether she had a job worth keeping after that.

CHAPTER EIGHT

ON THURSDAY morning, Amber had trouble holding back her nerves. Her stomach was fluttering, she felt shaky and full of doubt. If Zach hadn't already organized this she would never have gone ahead with the visit. But as it was, he turned up on the dot of ten o'clock and whisked her away, heading for town.

'You'll feel better once we get there and you have the chance to talk to Mrs Jennings,' he told her. 'I know you feel anxious and apprehensive right now, but it'll be all right, you'll see.'

'I hope so.'

Kate Jennings was a friendly, middle-aged woman, who welcomed Zach and Amber into her office and did her best to put Amber at ease straightaway. 'Let's start with coffee, and then we'll go through the file and see what we have in there,' she said.

The file was thin. 'There are some brief notes here,' Kate began. 'Your mother was an only child.

She was seventeen years old when you were born to her as a single parent, and it appears your father had little contact with you. She had been getting ready to start College in the autumn and her parents insisted that she found child care and went ahead with her education.' Kate looked at Amber briefly, conscious of the effect this information was having on her. 'Those first two years were very difficult for her, and she was under a lot of pressure, it seems, from all around. In the end, she was persuaded that her only course of action was to place you with a loving family.' Kate looked up. 'She married a couple of years after leaving College and has two other children now, but she says she would dearly love to have contact with you if you decide that's what you want.'

Amber absorbed that, trying to take it all in, wishing there was more and questioning what she'd been told. Her mother married and had other children? Yet she had given up her firstborn for adoption? How could she do that? She sat in silence for a moment, feeling abandoned all over again, until Zach reached over and covered her hand with his. 'She wants to see you, to talk to you,' he said. 'She probably didn't want to make the decision to place you for adoption, but felt she had no choice.'

Amber nodded. Finding her voice, she said quietly to Kate, 'What do I do now? I would rather meet her face to face than talk on the phone. How do I go about it?'

Kate smiled. 'I'll make some calls this morning to see if I can arrange a meeting, set up a time and place. Leave it with me and either way I'll be in touch, hopefully within the next few days.'

'Thank you.'

Amber left the office with Zach a few minutes later, and they walked out into the hot sunshine.

'Do you want to go somewhere for lunch, or maybe take a walk on the beach?' Zach asked. 'Or we could do both?'

'Perhaps we could take a walk, first,' she answered. 'I feel a bit strange. Sort of shell-shocked. I think I'd like to go somewhere quiet.'

'Okay.'

They drove to a sheltered beach along the coast, where Amber took off her shoes and walked with Zach over the firm sand, watching the waves roll on to the shore. She pointed out driftwood that had been washed up by the tide, glad of the diversion because her mind was in turmoil. 'I used to collect unusual pieces,' she told him. 'I'd make sculptures, like bonsai trees, or boats, and sometimes I would sell them at craft fairs. I wonder if any of my real family share that kind of interest?'

'Is there no one in your adoptive family who has an artistic flair?'

She shook her head. 'Not really. They're all very practical and straightforward, interested in business and in growing things. I'm different from them in a lot of ways. I like the seashore and countryside and animals, whereas they love exploring cities and don't really understand the need for having pets around. I sometimes feel as though I'm the cuckoo in the nest... well, I am, I suppose.' She sent him a fleeting glance. 'Don't get me wrong, I love my parents, and my brother, and we get on really well... it's just that we're very different people.'

'You get that even within natural families. My father loved the outdoor life, camping and trekking, and my mother went along with him, but she was happiest when she was home, cooking for the family, or at work at the hospital. She worked part time as a midwife and she said she loved it, loved seeing the newborn babies in their mothers' arms.'

'I can imagine how fulfilling that must be.' She was quiet for a while. How could a mother give up the child she'd held close to her heart and nurtured from that very first day?

'Oh, Amber… I've upset you,' Zach said, concern threading his voice as he saw her expression. 'I didn't mean to do that. I'm sorry – that was thoughtless of me. I'm so sorry.'

'It's all right. Don't worry about it. I'm just a little over-sensitive right now.'

He held her hand. 'The tide's coming in, so we should leave. Shall we go and find a café where we can sit for a while and have some lunch? There's been a lot for you to take in this morning and you might feel better with some food inside you.'

'Yes, all right.'

They found a café where they could sit behind a screen of potted palms and still look out of the window and watch the sea lap at the edges of the rocks. Zach ordered Mediterranean baked prawns with ciabatta and side salad for both of them, and they washed it down with chilled sparkling water.

Kate rang when they'd finished off their fruit sorbet desserts and were tasting the rich roasted coffee topped with a light swirl of cream. Amber looked nervously at her phone before answering the call.

'Good news,' Kate said cheerfully. 'Your mother was thrilled to bits to hear that you want to meet her, and she suggests tomorrow morning, if that's all right, at the Cliff Top hotel. She lives just a few miles from here, in Somerset, but she'll start out first thing. It'll take her about an hour and a half to get here, so she wants to know if you would meet about twelve o'clock and have lunch together?'

'Yes… yes, that's fine.' Amber finished the call a short time later, conscious that her hands were trembling a little. Glancing at Zach, she said, 'That was a quick result. I thought I might have to wait, or not get a response at all.'

He smiled. 'Do you want me to go with you tomorrow, for moral support? I could wait for you and pick you up after your meeting.'

She nodded. 'Would you? I'm feeling really anxious about all of this.'

'Of course. But I think you're probably worrying unnecessarily. It sounds as though your mother really wants to have some sort of relationship with you.'

'I know. But it might not work out – I have so many questions and she might not want to answer them. Where will that leave me, then?'

'Don't get ahead of yourself, Amber. You just have to take one step at a time.'

She subsided, sipping her coffee and absently savouring the chocolate mint that came with it. 'I should get back to the office,' she murmured after a while. 'There's a stack of work to get through, especially if I'm to be off tomorrow morning as well.'

'Don't worry about that. It'll do Liza good to feel her feet, see how to organize everything. Take the rest of the week off and concentrate on what matters most right now – your family. You might want to go and see your parents before they go away, and let them know what you're planning to do. Do you think they'll mind?'

'I'm not sure.' So, there was no place for her in the office. Zach had been good to her, but he'd also dragged the rug out from under her feet as far as work was concerned. Amber pulled in a deep breath. 'They've always been awkward about answering my questions, and I don't want to upset them, but this is something I have to do. I need to know who I am. And why I wasn't wanted.' She pushed her cup away. 'It was a good suggestion, though. I think I will go and see them.'

'Good.'

They left the café a short time later and Zach dropped her off at her apartment before heading for the office. No doubt he would spend the rest of the afternoon with Liza, but Amber wasn't going to dwell on that. It made her uneasy. Zach might deny that he was involved with her, but Liza clearly still felt possessive about him.

Instead, she busied herself, ringing her adoptive mother and then she headed over to the family home an hour or so later to have a heart to heart with her parents. It was never going to be easy, and they were shocked to hear that she was actually going ahead with the meeting, but she did her best to smooth things over. 'It's just something I have to do,' she told them. 'I have to know why I was given up. It'll haunt me all my life unless I find out the truth.'

She was up early on Friday morning, troubled about the forthcoming meeting and uncertain about what to wear. As if it mattered… her mother hadn't been there to see her choices over the last twenty-one years, so why did it matter now? In the end she settled for her best denim jeans and a camisole top. She felt comfortable that way, and that was one less thing to worry about.

Zach came to pick her up some half an hour before the meeting and guessed straightaway that she was a bundle of nerves. There was an aching feeling in her throat and her legs felt like jelly.

'You'll be fine,' he said. 'It'll all be over in an hour or two and then you'll know one way or another how you feel about going on with getting to know her.' He glanced at her as she slid into the passenger seat of his car. 'Have you remembered the party tonight at the Bayside Hotel? Rafael's looking forward to seeing you, to saying goodbye before he goes back to Spain.'

Would Zach be going there too, within a few weeks? Hadn't he said he was going to be spending some time overseeing the plans for the new project? Where did that leave her? 'Yes, I know about it.' She clicked her seat belt into place and he set off for the Cliff Top hotel, taking the coast road. She watched the landscape skim by, unaffected for once by the normally soothing vista of rolling hills and steep, wooded valleys, and the vivid blue of the sea. Zach talked to her throughout the journey, and she suspected he was trying to take her mind off things. It helped, and by the time they arrived at the hotel she was calm enough to step out on to the forecourt and take a deep breath.

'Call me when you're ready for me to come and fetch you,' he said.

'I will, thanks.'

She walked up the steps and into the foyer. 'I'm meeting someone here,' she told the girl at the desk. 'I'm Amber Kingston.'

'Ah, yes. The lady is already here. Adam will show you the way to your table in the restaurant.' She signalled to a uniformed young man standing by the pillared lounge.

'Thanks.'

Amber saw her mother almost straightaway, a lone woman sitting at a table by the window. She looked young, and she guessed she must be about forty years of age, a slender, attractive woman with blonde hair swept back in a stylish layered cut.

'Amber?' Livvy Halstead stood up as Amber approached, and it was clear that she was overcome by the enormity of the occasion. 'I've waited so long for this – I'm so glad you came, that we had the chance to meet after all this time.' She put out her arms to Amber, wanting to hug her, and Amber let her, feeling a little awkward, but at the same time glad of her mother's openness. Her mother's arms closed around her and it was as if she didn't want to let her go.

Eventually, they straightened and sat down at the table, each of them fighting their own chaotic emotions.

'I let things slide for a long while because I wasn't sure what to expect,' Amber said sitting opposite her mother. 'I wasn't convinced I was doing the right thing by trying to find you, and I didn't know if you'd want to see me. I thought you might have changed your mind.'

'Oh no… never. That would never happen. I was so desperate for this meeting to happen.' She hesitated, and after a moment or two Livvy picked up one of the menus the waitress had left and handed it to Amber. 'I'm so glad you went ahead and approached the Agency. I know you probably have a lot of questions – of course you do, you're bound to.'

'Yes, I do.' To cover their uncomfortable feelings, they studied the menu and laughed a little over the discovery that they both enjoyed similar foods. They chose a Cornish crab starter followed by tagliatelle with pork and spinach.

'Ask anything you like…' Livvy said. 'I don't mind. I've missed you so much, I just want everything to be right between us.'

Amber dipped a piece of crispy ciabatta into her crab salad and thought about what she wanted to say. Was there any point in beating about the bush? 'Most of all, I'd like to know why you gave me away. I was an infant, you had time to get to know me. Was I so much trouble that you couldn't keep me around?'

Livvy was shocked. 'Oh no… no, it was nothing like that. You must never think that. It was the worst day of my life when I signed the adoption papers. You were a perfect child. I loved you so much it was unbearable to part with you, but my parents insisted and made life difficult for me so that in the end I felt

I had no choice. They were very angry with me for getting pregnant. They said I was too young, they both had high flying careers and they didn't want the responsibility or the expense of looking after a young child while I was at College. They're not the sort of people who enjoy being around children – I expect that's why I'm an only child.' She paused to take a sip of water. 'I held off making the decision for as long as I could, and I looked into going it alone, but I didn't have money for rent and nursery care was too costly back then. My parents were paying my College fees. In the end, I was in despair about what to do. It broke my heart to let you go.'

'What about my father – didn't he have any say in it?'

Livvy shook her head. 'Leo was young, seventeen, the same as me, when we discovered I was pregnant. His family was shocked, because he was supposed to be going away to University to study, and this would set their plans right back. Both sets of parents tried to keep us apart.'

Amber toyed with the rest of her salad. 'So, you didn't see much of each other once the news was out?'

'Not much. We wrote, and phoned each other, and I told him about the way my parents were piling the pressure on me to go for adoption. I sent him photos of you. I was so upset. We were both upset. I didn't know how my parents could be so heartless, but they were never emotional people. They said it was for the best and I needed to get my life back on track.'

The waitress cleared away their dishes and returned a few minutes later with the main course. Amber and her mother talked about Amber's home life and her work, and whether she had any plans for the future.

Amber told her about someone else being given the job she'd worked for. 'I'm not sure where I go from here,' she said. 'I might look for work in Admin somewhere else. There must be other opportunities out there.' She dipped her fork into her pasta and glanced at her mother. 'Do you work? I know you have two children, so they must keep you busy.'

Livvy smiled. 'Luke is seventeen and Charlotte is fifteen, so they're fairly independent now. I studied art at College, and now I work as an art therapist with students who have problems like autism, mental health problems, or learning difficulties.' She sampled the tagliatelle and then took a sip from her chilled apple drink. 'I'd love it if you could meet your brother and sister. They would like it, too.'

Amber nodded. 'Yes, that sounds like a good idea. I'd like that.' She hesitated. 'Do you still keep in touch with my father? I think I'd like to get to know him, too.'

'Actually…that's not a problem. We married – a couple of years after I finished my College course.'

Amber gave a small gasp at this piece of news. 'You married each other?'

'Yes. We kept in touch even though we were separated, studying in different parts of the country. I'd left home for good by then – I couldn't bear to be there with all the memories - and Leo and I wanted to be together. We wanted to reverse the adoption, but of course that wasn't allowed, and by then it wouldn't have been fair to you to disrupt your life. Leo really wants to meet you, but he thought it might be too overwhelming for you to meet us both, today.'

'Yes, that's probably right. There's been so much to take in. I'm stunned, knocked for six by everything I've learned. But I'm so glad I've met you at last. It'll take me a while to get used to the idea that I have a whole new family.'

'We're only a short drive away – an hour and a half at most. You could come and stay with us one weekend, if you wanted.'

Amber nodded. 'Maybe I will. I'll look forward to it. And you could come and see me at Lake View, any time.'

They finished their meal with coffee, and then parted company, hugging each other and making arrangements to meet again the following week.

Amber waved her mother off and then called Zach to let him know she was ready to go home. He was there within minutes, coming to meet her in the foyer of the hotel.

'How did it go?' he asked, studying her for any sign of strain. 'Did you get on all right?'

'Yes, we did. I really like her.' She smiled. 'We're going to meet up again next week.' She touched his arm as they walked out to his car. 'Thanks for pushing me into this. I might have dithered for ever, if you hadn't started things off.'

'Hey, I'm glad it worked out all right.' He returned the smile. 'Do you feel better for seeing her?'

'I do. Somehow, I feel as though a weight's been lifted off me, and now I can breathe properly again.'

'I'm glad. I was hoping you would feel that way.'

She nodded. 'She's left me with a lot to think about. It's as though my whole world's been turned upside down, been shaken about… but in a good way. All my preconceptions have been blown away. I felt so sorry for her as a seventeen-year-old, faced with having a baby that her parents resented. It's hard to imagine people can be like that.'

'It is. But perhaps they've mellowed with time. They might have come to realize that their daughter's affection is something they don't want to lose.'

'Yes. Livvy did say that they make a point of coming to see her and the grandchildren at fairly regular intervals.'

'And now they'll see you, too.'

'I guess so.'

Dropping her off at the apartment a little later, he said, 'I'll see you later, at the party. I have to be there earlier than everyone else to make sure that everything's in order, but I'll send a car to pick you up. You will come?'

'Yes,' she said, but she wasn't altogether sure. Coming down from the high of finding her mother, she remembered with a jolt that her life was a roller-coaster ride, and she had no future to speak of, no defined title at work, and no confirmed place in Zach's life. He'd said himself he would be going away to deal with his projects abroad.

Perhaps he sensed her doubt. 'If you don't, I can always come and find you.' With that comment hanging on the air, he went back to his car and headed for the office.

CHAPTER NINE

THE THOUGHT of going to the party this evening, of being with Zach even for just a short time, sent a sudden, sharp thrill of excitement quivering through her, but it was an excitement that was mingled with sadness. Zach didn't love her. He wanted her, there was no denying that, but he had made it clear enough that he would never commit himself to any woman, and how could she bear to be with him and know that it all had to end, that she was only borrowing him for a short time? Could she stay with him on those terms?

There was Matt, too. What would Matt's reaction be if she should start an affair with Zach? He was her dear friend and the very last thing she wanted to do was to hurt him, yet how could she avoid it? She didn't know what he would do, but she didn't like to think that his bitterness might spill over to Zach and the two of them would end up hating each other. Look how heated they'd been over Matt's offer to take her away as his assistant. Two brothers warring with each other, all because she had crossed their path. She couldn't do that to either of them. She couldn't let it happen. Perhaps if she were to go away...

Zach's words echoed through her mind. Would he really come after her, if she didn't turn up at the Bayside Hotel? It wasn't very likely, but it might be better not to stretch the limits of possibility.

Perhaps after this evening's celebrations, she could simply slip quietly away, go to the coast maybe, to the cottage in Devon, where there would be no one to disturb her and she could try to come to terms with everything. She would have to find another job, of course, but she wasn't going to feel guilty about leaving her post in the Admin centre, not when Liza was firmly installed and well organized. What was the point in delaying? Her bags could be packed and ready, and she could be out of their lives before the night was through.

For the moment, though, there were other obligations that needed to be attended to. Rafael wanted to see her, he'd said, and then there was Matt, who surely deserved some kind of explanation before she went away.

Her mind was made up, and she hurried through her chores before starting to pack her bags. Tears shimmered in her eyes, but she dashed them away with the back of her hand as, for the second time in just a few days, she folded her things into her cases. Her heart was set on staying, but that would be her undoing. Being near Zach, seeing him every day, would be too much of a temptation to resist, would surely weaken her resolve and only prolong the agony.

She snapped the locks shut, and only when she was satisfied that everything was organized for her escape, did she think about getting ready for the evening ahead.

She put on a strawberry silk cocktail dress, adjusting the ruched bodice across the smooth slope of her breasts and checking the gentle drift of the skirt around her calves. There was no time now to do more than brush her hair vigorously and hope that the bright curls would settle into a semblance of order.

The taxi driver came for her in good time, dropping her off at the beach front hotel where Zach had hired a function room for the party. The double doors to the room were open, allowing a gently cooling breeze to drift through, and she walked in, hoping that she could circulate unobtrusively and then, in an hour or so, make her escape.

The atmosphere was noisy and lively, and there were people milling about in the main room and in the annexe, while others were propped up against the buffet tables, plates in hand as they talked and munched on a variety of canapés.

Zach was talking to Rafael and Matt, but although his back was to her as she walked into the lounge, he turned and looked at her, and she thought for a moment a bright spark of flame flared to life in his dark eyes.

'You're beautiful,' he greeted her, after excusing himself to Rafael and coming over to her. 'You look lovely. I'm glad you decided to come along to the party.'

'I came because I know this Spanish deal is important to you, and Rafael will be leaving tomorrow. Otherwise I might just have stayed home and thought about where I go from here on.'

'We need to get our heads together about that. I couldn't wait for you to get here... I wanted to be with you from the first moment – I wanted you all to myself, but this is an important evening, businesswise and I needed to be here.' He paused. 'Still, if you had decided to stay at home I'd have come and found you.'

'You'd hardly have deserted your guests to come in search of me,' she said evenly, but his mouth indented in a way that gave the lie to her words and set her heart thumping.

'Wouldn't I? If you believe that, then you have a lot to learn about me.' He took her hand and led her on to the small area that had been set aside for dancing. 'The DJ's playing a track that was made for us,' he murmured, sweeping her into his arms. The music swirled around them, the words of the romantic song filling her head like a dreamy love potion as they glided, intimately entwined, around the dance floor. 'I've been wanting to hold you like this for so long,' he said softly. 'I can't stop thinking about you.'

'Me, too,' she murmured. 'I think about you all the time. I don't seem able to help myself – I want to be with you.'

When the music came to an end he held her close, dropping a kiss gently on her lips. 'We can be together... there's nothing to stop us, is there?'

She looked up at him, the thrill of that kiss still trembling on her mouth. 'I don't know. I'm afraid, I think. I don't want to give my heart and have it crushed.'

'I wouldn't do that to you.'

'No? Maybe not intentionally.'

'I can see I'll just have to work harder to put your mind at rest,' he said. Glancing across the room they saw Rafael standing alone, a wine glass in his hand.

'Perhaps we should go over to him,' Amber suggested. 'It looks as though Matt's been called away to talk to someone else.' He was with a girl, Ted's sister, she guessed, helping her to choose food from the buffet table.

'Yes, we should. Come and say hello to the man. He's been waiting for you.'

They walked to the seating area where Rafael was looking around. The Spaniard clasped her hand warmly in his. '*Bueno*, Amber, it is good to see you again. My friend here has been keeping you busy, *es verdad*? I want to thank you for all the work you have done in the last few days. It has made life so much simpler for me.'

'*De nada*, Rafael, I was glad to help.' They talked for a while about the plans for the new Holiday Park, to be built on the Costa Brava. Rafael wanted to include a variety of water sports on site, as well as a restaurant with a terrace overlooking the sea.

'I expect Matt will be keen to help with that,' Amber said. 'He's very keen on designing restaurants and creating kitchen layouts.'

'I'm sure his help will be invaluable.' Rafael smiled at her. 'You've made life so much easier for me with all the translations of the documents you've prepared. I don't know how Zach will cope without you when he is in Spain over the next few months. Perhaps he will have to fax the documents to you.'

'He'll be gone that long?' Amber was surprised. Hadn't Zach said he was thinking of staying in Cornwall for some time?

'I'm sure we'll manage to sort something out,' Zach murmured, distracted momentarily by someone signalling him from across the room.

Liza was beckoning him with a slight wave of her hand. She had a businessman with her, someone Amber recognized as one of their suppliers. Zach frowned briefly, murmuring, 'Will you both excuse me? I think I'm needed at the bar.'

'Of course, you are much in demand this evening,' Rafael said with a nod. 'Do not worry about us. I shall take good care of Amber.'

'I'm sure you will.'   Drawing Amber to one side, Zach said in a roughened undertone, 'It's a nuisance, but there are bound to be a lot of interruptions like this. I have a certain amount of business to conduct this evening, but perhaps we can talk later, when everyone has gone.'

His hand circled her bare shoulder, the brilliance of his gaze compelling her to look up at him, and when she did, she knew that he was asking far more of her than his words implied. He wanted her, and if she was rash enough to succumb to his easy charm, he would make her his, for a few devil-may-care hours, or even weeks if she was lucky. Her heart turned over at the prospect. She wanted to stay, but deep down she knew she wouldn't be able to cope with the eventual collapse of their relationship when he grew tired of her. She had to steel herself to face that fact.

'I expect that's one of the hazards of attending functions like these,' she murmured, her blue gaze becoming withdrawn, distant. 'Work is never far away... you'd better go. Liza's looking anxious.'

His mouth made a straight line, his features shaded with some raw, dark emotion, before he said, 'I suppose you're right. I must.'

Rafael watched him go, then said, 'He has kept you under wraps, these last few days. He told me you had a great deal of work to do, but I suspect he wished to keep you all to himself. I can hardly blame him for that... but now at last I have my way. It is a pity I am to leave tomorrow, I should have liked to spend more time with you, but perhaps there is the chance that you will visit me in Spain, and enjoy my hospitality? Zach will bring you with him when he comes to my home, *sí?*'

'Thank you for the invitation, I'm sure I should like that.' Zach would probably have other ideas on that score, though, and she wasn't going to fool herself that she could ever play a major part in his social life. By the time he visited Rafael's home, she would be only a distant memory for him.

They spoke for a few minutes more, Rafael telling her about his house in Spain, and Amber describing for him the little village a few miles away from here where she'd been brought up. After a while, though, another guest claimed his attention, and she excused herself, to go and mingle with the crowd and chat with friends from Lake View.

Zach was caught up in the middle of a group of executives, but even from this distance, she was aware of his gaze shifting over her, burning on the edges of her vision as she moved about the room. She accepted a glass of wine from a passing waiter and slowly sipped the cool liquid.

Matt appeared at her side. 'Could we find a quiet corner somewhere?' he said, taking her hand and leading her towards a secluded table, screened by plants and a trellis. 'I want to talk to you.'

'About this business of the tour?'

'Yes, I meant what I said yesterday, you know. I want you to come with me.'

They sat down and she ran her fingers over the stem of her glass, thinking how to put into words what she needed to say.

'Matt, I can't,' she said simply. 'I think you should go on this tour, but I don't think it would work out if I went along with you.'

'Because of the way you feel about Zach?'

'For several reasons.' Her gaze was anguished, though, her blue eyes shimmering, because he had touched on a nerve. 'You knew all along, didn't you?'

Matt's shoulders lifted in a resigned gesture. He walked over to the window and stared out for what seemed like a long time. 'I guessed,' he said. 'I only had to see the two of you together, and I knew it had to happen. Are you in love with him?'

'Yes,' she said in a whisper. 'I think I am. The strange thing is, I don't know how it happened. One minute my life was fairly normal, everything was running along the usual course, and the next, wham, it all went haywire, as though I'd been struck by a force ten gale.' She gripped the seat of her chair, her fingers pressing tightly into the cushioned fabric. 'I'm sorry, Matt. If I could have changed things in any way, I would have. I didn't mean to hurt you.'

He turned back from the window, facing her. 'I know, Amber. I've known, almost from the beginning, that I didn't stand a chance with you.' His smile was rueful. 'At first I saw that as a challenge. I haven't been turned down that many times, you know, and you caught my interest right away. I was intrigued, I'd have done anything for you, anything to win you, and then slowly, everything seemed to turn upside down and my feelings began to change. I'm not sure what it is that I feel now, but it isn't the same. You've become a friend, a great friend to me, someone I can trust, someone I can feel at ease with.' His mouth gave a little twist. 'Unless you're annoyed, like yesterday, of course. I suppose I can understand now, why you were so upset. We're a selfish breed, we Berkeleys. We know what we want, and we go all out to get it, regardless of any other considerations. We're alike in that. I love my brother and I could never before imagine that I would fight him over anything, or anyone, but if he ever hurt you, I'd give him something to think about.'

His expression was fierce, and she said quickly, 'I don't want to see you arguing with him, especially not over me.'

'And I don't want you to suffer in any way because of Zach, but I'm afraid that you might. I won't stand by and watch it happen. I've seen him in action before, and I know he's never felt the need to settle down. He's too full of life and energy to want to be tied down, and he'll be on the move again, soon. I know for a fact that he's planning an extended trip to Spain sometime in the next few weeks to oversee the building work. With this new development coming up, he'll want to be on the scene.'

'Yes, I realize that. You don't need to warn me, Matt. He hasn't made me any promises that he can't keep, and I don't hold any expectations of any kind.'

'I'm thankful for that, at least. My offer still stands, you know.' He watched her keenly. 'You could come with me on this tour. No strings.'

She shook her head. 'I don't think so. Besides, Zach said my contract was binding. It would only cause more trouble between you.'

'I could weather that. The worst he could do would be to cause me financial problems, and I could deal with that. If he withheld my trust money, it would be a bit of a jolt to the system, but not fatal. I do have other income and qualifications enough to get another job. You'd be working for me.'

She gave him a tremulous smile. 'I'm not sure I deserve to have someone as nice as you for a friend,' she said. 'It was a lovely thought, but I really couldn't allow you to take any risks on my account.' Her mouth firmed as he made to object. 'No, I mean it. What I'd like to do is go away somewhere, to think things through and get some kind of perspective.' She hoped he would assume she meant to go just for a few days. She could give notice of leaving the job next week. 'I'd thought about leaving this evening, hiring a car and going down to the coast, to the family cottage in Devon.'

'That sounds as though you've already made up your mind.'

'I have. My cases are already packed, I was thinking of going right away, now that I've spoken to Rafael.'

'I'm glad you spoke to me first.' He took a deep breath and said, 'You're long overdue for some leave. Being by the sea will do you some good, I think, but you must let me drive you. There's no need for you to bother with the hassle of hiring a car at this time of night.'

'No, I don't want you do that. It's a two-hour drive. Besides, I think you should stay and keep Sarah company, I noticed her looking a little lost earlier, before your friend Ted swept her off to meet someone.'

'She'll be all right with Ted. I'll tell her where I'm headed. Anyway, last time I saw her she was with that crowd from Accounts. Come on, we'll slip away now while Zach's occupied.'

He pushed all her objections to one side and, in the end, she gave in, despising herself a little for her weakness. Arguing with him, though, would only cause more delay, and the more time went on, the more she was beginning to fret about getting away. If Zach knew what she was doing, he would try to stop her, and if that happened she would be lost.

They managed the first hurdle of leaving the hotel without any fuss, and Matt drove his car over to her apartment while she busied herself, sorting out last minute bits and pieces, and changing out of the cocktail frock and slipping on a simple button-through dress in its place. He stowed everything in the boot of his car, and to Amber's relief they were on their way within just a few minutes.

'I'll have to stop at the next service station,' he told her, when they had been on the road for some fifteen minutes. 'I need to fill up the tank.'

He pulled in at a garage about a mile further on, and she said, 'I'll get out and stretch my legs while you see to that.'

Matt filled up the tank and then went into the shop to pay the attendant, leaving Amber to slide out of the car and look around at the vista of rolling hills in the distance.

A moment later, she saw a car sweep on to the garage forecourt, and then she bit back a gasp as she recognized the familiar shape of the gleaming Lotus and watched it swerve to a halt in front of Matt's SUV.

The door swung open and Zach climbed out, striding towards her, his features taut.

'Amber, would you tell me what's going on?' The quietness of his tone made her face lose all its colour.

'Zach, what are you doing here?' she said. 'Shouldn't you be with your guests? Surely you shouldn't have left them to fend for themselves? What will people think?'

'I don't much care what people think,' he answered. His glittering, raking glance swept over her, taking in the light swirl of her dress, the smooth golden expanse of throat and shoulders left vulnerable to the cool drift of the evening air. 'Do you mind telling me what you're doing here?'

'Zach, you might be my employer but that doesn't give you the right to enquire into what I do with my free time.'

'You know this has nothing to do with our work relationship,' he said. 'But if you want to go down that route, as your employer, I think I have every right to expect you to remain at a business function until the end. Perhaps you didn't read the small print of the contract you signed?'

His remarks left her flustered for a moment. It had been so long ago, she couldn't remember exactly what had been in the small print, but she ventured, 'I do recall that it wasn't signed in blood. From the look on your face, though, perhaps that's something you'd like remedied?'

'What I'd like,' he said, 'is to know why you've taken off in the middle of the night. I thought we were getting on so well together. You know how much I wanted to spend time with you – I thought you felt the same way.'

The grim set of his jaw strained her outward composure, and when he approached her she stepped nervously back. She could see the tension in his body, the flickering uncertainty in his eyes, and she swallowed against the aching constriction in her throat.

'I really appreciate what you did for me today,' she said carefully, 'but I didn't agree to stay. You asked me to come along to say goodbye to Rafael, and I've done that. Zach, I don't see any future for you and me – you've never wanted to stay with one woman for any length of time, you told me so, and that's not the kind of set-up I want for myself. I'm through with being hurt and left behind. I'm sorry.'

His gaze shifted over the silken sweep of her skin, the curve of her breasts outlined by the perfect fit of the bodice. 'I think you could at least give me an explanation of why you're here with Matt. But I really don't need to be told, do I? It's clear enough what you're doing together. You were in such a hurry to leave with him, you didn't want me to know.'

'Yes, I was in a hurry,' she agreed, injecting a crisp vitality into her tone that bore no relation to the way she was feeling. 'I'm going away for a while, to the cottage in Devon, and I'd very much like to get there before morning. Matt said he would drive me there.'

'You know it's unwise to go anywhere with my brother. That would be a mistake.'

Matt came over to them. 'Isn't that for Amber to decide? If she wants to go away, there's no reason why anyone should stop her.'

'I have reason enough,' Zach retorted. 'I can't stand by and watch her go off with you. Apart from any other reservations I might have, you've already had two near misses on the roads in the last few weeks, and you were drinking earlier on this evening. I'm warning you now, Matt, if you attempt to take her any further I shall stop you.'

Matt's shoulders squared, and Amber suddenly saw all her fears coming home to roost. She had to put an end to this, quickly. Her mouth firmed.

'Zach, you're making a big issue out of this, and there's no need to do that. I'm going to spend a few days by the sea, hardly any distance at all, and Matt has offered to drive me there. He's hardly touched any alcohol, he's had plenty to eat to soak up what he's had, and I'm sure he's perfectly capable of taking me where I want to go.' She drew in a ragged, determined breath. 'I'm sorry if you don't like my plans, but that's the way things stand. I've made up my mind, and you'll just have to deal with it the best way you can.'

She started to walk back towards the SUV, but found herself stopped in her tracks by the gentle but firm clasp of Zach's hand on her arm. 'I'll do that,' he informed her tersely. 'And since your mind's so definitely made up, I think I should be the one to take you where you want to go.' He turned to Matt. 'Perhaps you ought to go and make sure that Sarah's all right. She's been asking for you, waiting for you to go back – I know you told her where you were going, but she and Ted are there at your invitation, remember? I think she's feeling a little neglected.' And to Amber he added, 'Will you let me drive you?'

She looked at his brother. 'Matt,' she said, 'is Sarah really waiting for you?'

He looked sheepish. 'Uh… probably. I wasn't thinking clearly when we set off. It was all a bit rushed.' Her might-have-been saviour didn't look at all as though he was about to leap into action. In fact, he hadn't moved a single centimetre. He was just standing there, looking bemused. 'I suppose I ought to go and see that she's okay.' He frowned. 'Your cases are in the boot of my car.'

'Then we'd better transfer them to mine, don't you think?' Zach said, then looked at Amber. 'Will you let me do that?'

She nodded, and a few minutes later she was seated beside him in the Lotus. She waved goodbye to Matt, and then sat silently for a while, contemplating the turn of events.

Zach turned the car on to the main road. 'Is this getaway a spur of the moment thing?'

'Yes. Sort of. I just felt I needed some space to think things through.'

'Hm… this is your birthday weekend, isn't it?'

'It is. I thought I might head for the cottage in Devon. I want to spend some time on the beach, sorting things out in my head. I have a key, and obviously no one else is going to be using it over the next few days.'

'Okay, give me directions and we'll head over there.' She told him and he set the address in the satnav. He switched on the radio and soft music drifted out of the speakers, filling the car with a calming melody. Then he glanced obliquely at her. 'It'll take a couple of hours to get there, so you may as well relax, enjoy the ride in comfort.'

Amber nodded, but she was silent, deep in thought. Why was he doing this? True, he'd cared enough to help her find her mother, but it wasn't as though his feelings for her went deep down, was it? The reality was, she was just another passably attractive female who'd caught his attention, a little secretary who would help him pass his time at the Holiday Park in a pleasant fashion.

When he turned off the coast road a few minutes later, she strained to follow the route, but darkness had fallen and it was hard to make out the landscape.

Eventually, he changed course on to a winding, narrow track, and she stared straight ahead as he swung through an arched gateway and a building loomed up out of the shadows in front of them.

'Here we are,' he said. 'Your cottage by the sea.'

CHAPTER TEN

ZACH PARKED the car and switched off the ignition. 'Shall we go into the house?'

The stone-built cottage was shrouded in darkness, and it was hard to make out the path, but Zach's hand was firm and supportive on her arm as he led her over the flagstones. Inserting her key in the lock of the solid front door, she pushed it open and flicked on the light switch, leading the way along the wood tiled hallway into the lounge.

There was an oak floor in here, too, complemented by the cheerfulness of warm, cream and rose-tinted furnishings, golden oak shelving units and a display cabinet filled with crystal cut glassware. The window drapes were rose-coloured, adding to the gentle homeliness of the room. There were deep-cushioned arm chairs close by the fireplace, and in one corner of the room there was a book case, its shelves lined with volumes that she remembered from her childhood.

'This is a lovely room,' Zach said, looking around.

'Yes, it's a room to curl up in and pass long, lazy evenings.' For just a moment Amber wondered what it would have been like if she could have looked forward to any of those blissful evenings with Zach, but then she let it go. The thought made her feel intolerably sad, and a small sigh of unhappiness quivered on her lips. It wasn't to be, and there was no point in idle imaginings, was there? They only made reality seem infinitely more painful.

'I'll put the heating on,' she said, glancing at him. 'That should take the chill off the place.'

'Good idea. It was warm back at the hotel, but you're not dressed for any sudden change in temperature.'

'No, maybe not,' she said, conscious of his grey-blue eyes taking in every detail of the pale blue-toned dress that clung to her curves and swirled gently around her slender legs. 'I made up my mind to come here at the last minute. I wasn't really thinking clearly.' She frowned. 'All my things are in the car – but what will you do? I'm assuming you don't want to drive back tonight?'

'I'd sooner stay, if that's all right with you?'

She thought about it. 'I think there may be some of Nico's clothes in his room upstairs. He's tall, like you, and a similar build.'

'Thanks, maybe I'll take a look later.'

She nodded. 'You could use his room while you're here. It's all made up, ready. I came down here last weekend to make sure everything was in place for the family.'

His eyes darkened. 'I'm sorry things didn't turn out for you the way you wanted.'

195

She lifted her shoulders. 'It couldn't be helped, I suppose.' As an afterthought, she said, 'Are you hungry? I didn't see you eat anything at the hotel, and I wouldn't mind something more substantial myself.'

He frowned. 'I think I am.' He looked surprised. 'I haven't given a thought to food for several hours, but all at once I'm ravenous.'

'Good,' she said, and he smiled, a warm, attractive lift to his mouth that had her insides turning to marshmallow. 'Do you think you might like beef with red wine topped with sliced potato?'

He nodded, looking surprised. 'Is that possible?'

'Yes, I made a hot-pot for the family when I was over here and put it in the freezer. There's apricot crumble, too. It won't take too long to heat them up.'

'Is there anything I can do to help?'

'You could pick out a bottle of wine from the rack. Come on, I'll show you the kitchen.'

This was another homely room, fitted out with cupboards built of golden oak, and a range of equipment that would have been a chef's dream.

'This is a lovely house,' he said quietly. 'It's odd, though, that it looks so very well cared for, and lived in, when I don't suppose you get to stay here very often?'

'That's true, but we come here whenever we get the chance, especially in the Spring and Summer.' She switched on the central heating, then set the oven to heat and took out the prepared hot-pot from the freezer. 'A woman from the village comes in once a week to give the place a dust over, and she gets supplies in for us when she knows we're due to spend any time here.'

'That sounds like a sensible arrangement.'

'It works for us.' She sent him a quick glance. 'I don't suppose you ever feel the need to get away and wind down. From what I've heard, you thrive on keeping busy, being constantly on the move.' As she spoke, she set about making a quick salad from ingredients in the fridge.

Zach picked out a bottle of red wine and hunted around for glasses. 'I need to relax, like anyone else. It's just that travelling around has become a way of life. It's what I'm used to. It's what I've had to do to build the business.'

'And Matt will do the same, I expect. Going on this tour is just the beginning, isn't it?'

'It's what he wants.' He found a corkscrew and opened the bottle.

'But he doesn't always get what he wants, does he? After all, he wanted me to go with him, but you put a stop to it.'

'Because I didn't want to lose you.'

She frowned, conscious of him watching her as she put plates in the oven to warm. 'It wasn't a business decision, then?'

'No. It was purely a gut reaction. I wanted you to be with me.' She looked up at that, her eyes widening.

Zach shrugged. 'Anyway, he'll find another assistant easily enough. Sarah's keen to go with him. She's very competent and I expect she'll jump at the chance to act as his personal assistant. When he's been away from you for a while he'll begin to get a grip on himself and think things over more clearly. Then he'll perhaps see the sense in taking her along.

He likes her. I don't think he'll take much persuading.'

Amber was still mulling over the fact that he wanted her enough to stop her going away, but she said quietly, 'I think you have the wrong idea about Matt and me. We get along well, and maybe he wanted more than that at the beginning but, the truth is, we're just good friends.' His brows lifted at that and she added, 'I should have made it clear to you before this, but you riled me.' Her mouth made a crooked line. 'I suppose you've already put the idea to Sarah, haven't you?'

He smiled. 'It might have come up in the course of conversation.'

The oven timer pinged and she took the plates from the oven and set them out on the oak table. 'The food's ready now,' she told him, placing the hot casserole dish at the centre. 'Help yourself.'

'Thanks.' He sat down opposite her and spooned the tender meat and vegetables on to his plate, adding a topping of crispy potatoes. 'Mm... this smells good,' he murmured. He dipped his fork into the hot casserole and savoured the taste on his tongue. 'This is delicious,' he said. 'The best I've tasted in a long time.'

She smiled. 'I'm glad.'

He studied her briefly as he poured wine for both of them. 'Is this the kind of thing your mother makes – your adoptive mother?'

She nodded. 'Yes. She taught me a lot about cooking.' She took a mouthful of the herb infused vegetables. 'It's awkward,' she mused, 'knowing how to distinguish between my mother and my birth mother. Livvy said it was up to me to decide what I wanted to choose to call her and she'll go along with my choice. I'm sort of trying out Mum in my mind.'

'Are you okay about her reasons for letting you go?'

'I think so. She was very young, and it sounds as though her parents were quite unsympathetic towards her. They didn't want her to go ahead with the birth but she refused to do as they asked. I don't think she sees an awful lot of them nowadays – mostly because they're quite remote personalities, and they travel a lot on business and so on, though they do see their grandchildren whenever they're home.'

'Sometimes you have to travel to keep up the business interests.'

'Hm.' She cleared away the plates and served the apricot crumble, adding a dish of whipped of cream to the table. 'Have you discounted the idea of ever having children, a family of your own?'

He brooded on that for a moment or two. 'Until recently I hadn't thought much about it. Work has always been uppermost in my mind.'

'But now you're having second thoughts?' A small ray of hope started up in her. 'How would you be able to give your children the attention they need if you're constantly on the move?'

'I guess I'd have to learn to delegate. I'm sure there are some talented, well-qualified people who could be trusted to run things for me. I'd have to become an overseer, checking up on the state of play from time to time.'

Her mouth curved. 'Do you really think you could take a back seat?'

His gaze meshed with hers. 'Given the right incentive, yes.'

Warm colour flooded her cheeks. Was he really saying she might be his reason for changing his way of life? Flustered, she stood up and began to make coffee, while Zach cleared the dishes and stacked them in the dishwasher.

'Shall we take the coffee into the lounge?' she suggested, and he nodded, opening the door for her to allow her go through with the tray.

He sat down beside her on the sofa, their coffee on the table in front of them. 'I'm glad you let me bring you here tonight,' he said. 'This evening started off like one of my worst nightmares. I spent what seemed like hours making polite conversation with people, when all I really wanted was for everyone to leave so that I could be alone with you. That was bad enough, but seeing you slip out of the hotel with Matt did something to me. Something shattered. When I found out from Ted and Sarah that you were going away together it was like being hit in the stomach, it was a physical pain, and I couldn't think beyond the fact that I had to come after you.'

She said cautiously, 'I wasn't going away with him. He was just helping me out -'

'Yes.' He frowned. 'But you weren't intending to come to the coast for a few days, were you, no matter what you told Matt? There was something more. I knew it, I felt it. It had to be that you were planning on staying away, you were walking out on me, for good.' He looked at her, his eyes dark. 'Why, Amber? Why would you do that?'

She was troubled, trying to find a way to explain. 'You'll be going away yourself, to Spain, for several weeks. Rafael told me so, and you'd mentioned it some time ago -'

'Yes, but -'

'And I didn't want you fighting with your own brother because of me. There's been a lot of tension between you lately, but you're right, Matt thought I was taking a few days holiday to think things through.' She paused to gather her thoughts and went on more slowly, 'In fact, I'd made up my mind to leave you both. I didn't want to be the cause of any problems between you. I wasn't sure what I felt for him to begin with, except for friendship, and then you came along, and I was completely bewildered. I'd never experienced anything like the feelings I have for you, and when you two started arguing in the office I knew that I had to sort it all out.'

'By leaving?'

'What point was there in staying? You aren't one for commitment, and I need that. I've spent my life feeling as though I was abandoned, not wanted, always coming second best, and I'm not looking to get involved with someone who will walk out on me after a few weeks, or months. I needed space, time to think. Coming here and getting away from it all was the best option.'

'No... no, it wasn't, Amber.' He drew her close to him, his arms enclosing her. 'How could it ever have been the best way? And how was I supposed to find you again? It could have taken a team of investigators weeks to pinpoint your whereabouts.'

'You weren't supposed to find me. I just wanted to spend some time at the beach, sorting out my thoughts. You wouldn't really have hired anyone, would you?' She looked at him uncertainly, and his dark eyes took on a diamond bright glitter.

'Of course, I would have. I couldn't bear to think that you were somewhere in this world and that I couldn't see you, be with you. I've never felt that way about any woman before.' He kissed her fiercely, the tension in him bunching the muscles of his arms, tightening the hard length of his body. 'Please don't ever do this to me again, Amber,' he muttered. 'I need you. Promise me that you'll stay, or I'll never know a moment's peace.'

She hardly dared hope that he cared for her as much as his words implied. He had been shocked, and impelled into action at the thought of losing her, but that might just be a momentary thing, a fleeting passion that would fade with the morning. It was something she didn't want to face.

For now, though, she was in his arms, and she would be content with that. She had no more will to fight against the temptation of being with him. She was lost to all the cries of common sense, and she would stay with him, allow herself the joy of loving him, until he was the one to call a halt.

'I promise I won't leave you,' she whispered, 'not for as long as you want me.'

His answering kiss devoured her, took everything that she had to give, and when his lips finally broke free of her mouth, it was only so that they could trace a lingering, sensual pattern over the vulnerable curve of her throat and the soft, smooth line of her shoulders. 'I want you,' he muttered thickly. 'I've wanted you from that very first day.'

The tension was still there, in every flicker of muscle, in the shadowed planes of his face, the firm, hard line of his mouth. She lifted a hand to touch his jaw, wanting to soothe away the edge of strain, and glorying in the feel of his male skin beneath her finger tips. He turned his head, and his mouth claimed her palm, kissing her, nipping her fingers one by one.

She gave a soft moan, leaning into him, the softness of her curves merging with his hard body, but it wasn't enough, being close was not nearly enough. She wanted more, she wanted the swift urgency of his lovemaking, the crushing pressure of his arms around her. Yet he was moving away and she was totally confused.

He took her with him, gripping her hand in his own, taking her up the stairs and into the bedroom with that very urgency she had craved, pushing the door shut behind them with the flat of his hand. Dizzily, as though in a dream, she went into his welcoming arms, and he kissed her, possessing her with his mouth until her body trembled with need.

His hands shaped her, caressed, stroked, and when she moved against him, the buttons of her dress loosened under the bidding of his subtle fingers. The dress slid to the floor, leaving her in only satiny wisps of underwear, and he gave a harsh groan, his eyes brilliant with heated passion as they shifted over her. Her own hands began a tentative exploration, curving around his shoulders as his palm made a slow glide along her spine and drove her to move against him in sensuous desire.

Her breasts firmed in instant response to the sweet friction, her whole body suddenly charged, tingling with excitement. He kissed her again, his fingers moving against the clip of her bra, releasing it, smoothing over what was left of her flimsy satin covering, until that, too, fell away. Easing her backwards, he tipped her gently on to the bed, and switched on the lamp, filling the room with a soft golden glow.

'I need to see you,' he murmured, and a whisper of uncertainty sounded in her head as he looked down at her. How could she compare with the women he had known before? How could she ever hope to please him? She had known nothing of love and passion before this, her only experience was the fierce, aching need she felt for him, but it couldn't be enough, not when there had been others before her, other women who knew everything there was to know.

He was removing his own clothes, and she said raggedly, 'I wish I could be everything you wanted. I wish-'

'You're lovely,' he said, his voice a low rumble in his throat as he came down beside her. 'You're beautiful, exquisite, and I need you so badly I think I've been going out of my mind with wanting you.'

'But what if I disappoint you? What then?'

'Sweetheart, what are you talking about? How could you possibly disappoint me?' His hand gently traced the line of hip and thigh, then swept upwards to tenderly caress the rounded fullness of her breast. He looked into her eyes and read her uncertainty and said, 'What are you saying? Are you trying to tell me that this is your first time, that you've never made love with anyone before?' His eyes were smoky with doubt.

'I've never made love before,' she whispered. He was stunned, she knew, because he stiffened at her words. She said unhappily, 'Does it make a difference?'

'Of course. Yes,' he said huskily, and all the tension left him as he moulded her to him. 'It makes a difference. It means you will be mine, and I shall adore you and protect you, and take you slowly and thoroughly, and show you all there is to know about the pleasure your body can experience. I had no idea… I never dreamed…'

His mouth captured hers, his caressing fingers leading her into golden realms of ecstasy, and for a long, long while after that there was only delight and exhilaration and the sheer joy of knowing what it could be like to have the man she loved treat her with such tender absorption. He worshipped her with his hands and lips, his questing mouth discovering every sweetly aching part of her body and bringing it to feverish, hectic life. He roused in her a restless, tormented need that only he could slake, and she whimpered softly, smothering her cries in the warm curve of his shoulder until she could bear it no longer.

'Zach, please-'

'Soon, my angel.' He moved over her, his body golden in the lamplight, and she gazed on him in wonder, running her hands over the muscled perfection of his chest and his hard, flat stomach.

'But I want you now-' It was a breathless demand that brought a laugh of husky satisfaction to his lips, but still he teased and caressed, circling deliciously on the centre of her need, until she writhed in heedless abandon.

Only then did he test the barrier of her womanhood and slowly thrust, his body shuddering with desire as he possessed her. Her stunned gasp hovered on the air and his eyes darkened as he fought for control. His mouth brushed hers, a feather-like, fleeting contact, and after a moment he began to move once more, building the throbbing rhythm until sensation after sensation exploded inside her and she was flung into an exhilarating world of pleasure that she had never imagined could exist. He followed her there, the sounds of satisfaction thick in his throat, and they drifted together, tossed on that whirlpool of exquisite sensuousness for endless moments before they drifted into the languid journey back to normality.

He held her still, his limbs stretching and tangling with hers in lazy contentment, and she succumbed to the unspoken invitation, curling into his embrace and closing her eyes as the sweet lassitude enveloped her. Wrapped in each other's arms they slept.

When she woke, pale sunlight was casting dancing beams on to the walls of the room, and she blinked cautiously, looking around for Zach as memory returned. She was alone, covered by a light duvet, and she realised that at some point in the night Zach must have laid it over her. The thought warmed her as she made her way to the ensuite bathroom.

When she returned to the bedroom, there was the scent of coffee on the air, wafting in through the open door. She wrapped herself in the duvet and Zach appeared with a tray, setting it down on a table. She sat on the bed, holding on to her covering, because in the light of morning the knowledge of her nakedness was unsettling. He was already dressed, in dark denims that moulded his strong thighs, and a navy tee shirt that emphasised his broad shoulders. She drank in his fluid, efficient movements, not wanting to take her eyes off him for a moment.

'I thought you might like some coffee and toast,' he said, planting an unexpected kiss on her soft mouth and leaving her quivering with need and an overwhelming sense of loss when he lifted his head.

'That was thoughtful of you,' she murmured absently, ignoring the tray as her gaze drifted hungrily over him.

'At least this will keep you going until we get a proper breakfast. I thought you might like to head for the beach. It's another glorious day.'

'Is it?' She blinked, gathering her wits. 'I must get dressed,' she said, and was about to stand up until she remembered her cases in the boot of Zach's car. Feeling oddly shy, she stopped and said, 'What am I going to wear?'

Zach considered her for a second or two, then suggested with a crooked grin, 'How about a towel?'

A flush of pink stole across her cheeks, and his grin turned to a husky laugh. 'It's all right, I brought your cases in from the car.' His brilliant gaze shimmered over her once more, lingering on the pale gold of her arms, and the smooth slope of her breast where the duvet was slipping. 'I suppose you must dress, though I must admit I'd much prefer seeing you wander about the place in what you're wearing now.'

'I'm shocked,' she said, admonishing him with glinting eyes. 'I was brought up to be a nice girl, a good girl.'

'And you are,' he murmured, coming to sit beside her on the bed. 'Absolutely delightful.' His arms came around her, and she pressed her cheek into the smooth muscle of his chest, her finger tips pressed against the thin material of his shirt. 'I'd like to spend forever and a day with you.'

She laughed. 'You're in no rush to get back to Cornwall, then?'

'Not now that the Spanish deal is signed and sealed. The actual development work and all that goes with it can wait for a few weeks.' His hand stroked the silk of her hair, tangled in the curls at her nape.

'We could stay here for more than just a weekend. My family are all away now.'

'So, we could use this house as a base to go out and about, if you want?'

'Yes.' She wanted to be wherever he was. She would live forever on the memories, if that was all she could have. 'Is that what you had in mind for me back at the office? More work on the Spanish development?'

'Something like that. I had the idea we could work together on that. And, of course, I expect you'll want to be there to see to the setting up of the wild life area, and so on.'

She looked up at him. 'Do you mean you're going ahead with it? I thought you wanted to build a pool and sun lounge.'

'I still do. But there's no reason why another pool can't be fitted in somewhere on the South side of the Park. It just means the layout will have to be chosen more carefully to blend in with what's already there. I think you have some sound ideas, along with a good head for organization – that's why I decided you'd make a first-class personal assistant for me, not for Matt.'

She swallowed carefully against the sudden ache in her throat. He wanted her as his assistant. He'd planned a role for her in his life after all, and even if it was just a tiny part, it had to be better than nothing.

'So, you've thought it all through.'

'Mostly. I wasn't sure that it was fair to ask you to travel with me, but it seems to me you might not be entirely against the idea, and I think maybe I could find a solution to everything. It will mean living in Spain for a while. Would you mind that?'

'I… uh-' Her voice caught in her throat, and she started again. 'No… I've spent a lot of time there, with my parents.'

'That's what I thought. You could meet up with them over there from time to time. And of course see your birth family when we're home.' He hugged her close, his hands clasping around her. 'Of course, as you pointed out, we'll have to organize things a little differently if we decide to start a family of our own, but by then I should be able to hand over to others more, and we could always arrange to do our travelling around in the holidays.'

'Wait - wait a minute,' she said, placing the flat of her hand on his broad chest. 'Slow down a minute, you're going way too fast for me on this.'

'Am I?' He frowned. 'Didn't you want children? I assumed - I took it for granted, knowing you, seeing how-'

'Yes, yes,' she said impatiently. 'Back up a bit, will you? I've managed to get as far as the personal assistant, and the travel bit, but you lost me somewhere after that,'

'Did I?' He gave her a puzzled, searching glance. 'Isn't it the natural course of events when two people love each other... to get married? I know a lot of couples live together these days, but I couldn't settle for that, not with you. I want to know that you're mine, that we're committed to each other for as long as there is. And I know you need that reassurance, too. Isn't that true?'

'You love me?' she whispered, her blue eyes very wide. 'You really love me?'

'Of course, I do. You must know that I do. Why do you think I got all steamed up and came after you? Even Matt recognized that.'

'Matt did? How do you know?'

'He said this morning when I phoned him that he'd never seen me in such a state, and he'd never known me go after any woman before this, and that it had to be the real thing.'

'But you didn't say. You didn't tell me,' she murmured, dazed. 'Not once.'

'Didn't I? I thought I showed you, last night, how much I love you?'

'Ye-es, but…' She faltered. 'That was… I mean, for me it was something very, very special, but for you… well, there have been others and…'

'It was special for me, too,' Zach interrupted, 'because I was making love to you, to the woman I love. I never felt this way before. I feel as though I've been through a hurricane and come out stronger. I want to cherish and protect you and keep you by me for ever. Don't you feel something of that?'

She lifted a hand to touch his face. 'I love you,' she said, 'but I was so afraid of losing you. I was afraid that you might only want me for a little while and then I'd be devastated when you left me. I was such a coward, I didn't think I could bear the pain of losing you.'

He bent his head to crush her lips beneath his own and she clung to him, winding her fingers around his neck, and feeling the strength in his taut muscles.

'I won't ever hurt you,' he muttered. 'You must believe me.'

'I believe you,' she said huskily, kissing him, and he tilted her back into the pillows, sliding his hand beneath the duvet to stroke her warm skin.

'Will you marry me, Amber?'

'Yes…' She smiled, her heart swelling with love. 'Yes, I will.'

He breathed a sigh of relief and satisfaction. 'I never thought this could happen to me,' he said, kissing her gently, wrapping his arms around her. 'I love you so much.'

'I love you,' she said, running her hands lightly down his back. 'I want to be with you, always.'

'And you will. We'll always have each other. All I want is to make you happy.' He thought about that for a moment. 'I suppose,' he murmured thickly, with more than a hint of resignation in his voice, 'we should be getting ready to go to the beach. You did say you wanted to go there today.'

'Did I?' She stretched sinuously under the lazy, tantalizing caress of his fingers. 'There's always another day, though, isn't there? We said we might stay longer.'

'We did, didn't we?' He smiled into her eyes and his hand strayed to cup the heavy fullness of her breast. 'Of course, you might want to go downstairs and get some breakfast. I expect the coffee and toast I made must have gone cold by now.' Again, there was that slight hint of reluctance in his tone.

'Mm...' She ran her hand over his chest, felt the heavy beat of his heart jerk in response beneath the fabric of his tee shirt. 'You're probably right.' Her fingers traced delicate whorls on the thin material. 'But I think I'd much rather stay here. Didn't you say, one time, that you were going to lay in a stock of these?'

His hard body stirred as she stretched with sensuous indolence, her long limbs moving against his. 'Stock of what?' he asked. 'Tee shirts?'

'And jeans. As I recall, you said that you might take to wearing them, so that you could get a little rumpled... and it just occurred to me... since we have time on our hands...' She let the sentence trail away.

'Oh, definitely,' he said, laughing softly as he read her mind and held her close. 'By all means rumple me a little...'

* * * * *

Printed in Great Britain
by Amazon